IN THY TENDER CARE

IN THY TENDER CARE

COURTNEY RANGER

This book is a work of fiction. Names, characters, businesses, organizations, places, events, and incidents either are the product of the author's imagination or are used fictitiously. Any resemblance to actual persons, living or dead, events, or locales is entirely coincidental.

Quotes from *A Christmas Carol* by Charles Dickens, 1843

Printed in the United States of America.

Cover design by Mountain Peak Edits & Design
Editors : Miriam and Samantha

First Edition: October 2025
Paperback ISBN : 978-1-970375-00-8

*To those who make our Christmases merry, even
when it's hard.*

Away in a Manger

Away in a manger, no crib for a bed,
the little Lord Jesus laid down His sweet head;
the stars in the heavens looked down where He lay,
the little Lord Jesus asleep on the hay.

The cattle are lowing, the Baby awakes,
but little Lord Jesus, no crying He makes.
I love Thee, Lord Jesus, look down from the sky
and stay by my side until morning is nigh.

Be near me, Lord Jesus; I ask Thee to stay
close by me forever, and love me, I pray.
Bless all the dear children in Thy tender care,
and fit us for heaven, to live with Thee there.

T a b l e   o f   C o n t e n t s

Prologue

I **could still see it plain as day.**

The boy falling from the tree. The sickening crack as his head hit the ground. The blood that gushed from his head, that had stained my hands. The panicked attempt to save him. The doctor's eyes boring into me as he wordlessly informed me his so-called skills were worthless to save the child I'd come to love. The doctor's emotionless voice as he informed the boy's mother. The mother collapsing to the ground as she let out an inhuman shriek.

I swiped at the tears running down my face, trying to regain some semblance of composure. I would've thought that a whole year would have been enough time to recover, but the pain was still there, as sharp as ever.

"Johnny, I miss having you in my class. You were such a little light. I-I'm-I'm so sorry." Once again, I swiped at the tears clouding my vision.

"I remembered that you liked Christmas wreaths, so I made a special one just for you," I said as I placed the small circle of evergreen boughs next to the wooden cross. "I-I know it isn't perfect, but I..."

A twig snapped, and I whirled around to face the intruder. Standing just a few paces behind me was the person I'd be perfectly content never to see again. The doctor.

The one responsible for the boy's death.

One

What had possessed Frankie, the worst student in my class, to gift me an apple, I didn't know, but I was much too eager for food to care. I'd had to stay longer after class than expected, so while I worked on tidying up the schoolhouse before I left, I was grateful to have some sort of snack.

I lifted the fruit to my lips, eager for its juicy sweetness.

"I wouldn't," a male voice stated.

I whirled around. The doctor stood in the entrance to the classroom, his tall, confident form inspiring the greatest sense of irritation in me. Must the infernal man intrude *everywhere*? There certainly was no call for a doctor in *my* schoolhouse, especially since all the children had already gone home.

"And why, may I ask, is that?" I shot back.

"It looks like it's already being enjoyed."

Confused, I turned the apple in my hands and saw the tell-tale mark of a worm feasting on the apple. I flinched when I saw it, dropping the apple on instinct.

The fruit had the audacity to roll toward the doctor, stopping at his feet. He picked it up and walked it to the wastebin.

I tried to ignore the flush heating my cheeks. "May I ask why you are intruding on my schoolroom?"

Instead of answering, he gestured to the wall behind me. I turned and saw Frankie and a few other students peeking through the window at me, all laughing. Once they saw me watching, they turned and started running.

I stuck my head out of one of the open windows and shouted after the incorrigible boy, "Frankie! You'll be staying after school tomorrow to clean blackboards for me! And don't think I won't tell your mother!"

"Actually," the doctor started. I wheeled around, having totally forgotten my audience. "No, he won't be."

"And who are you, may I ask, to tell me how I should and should not run my classroom?"

"Ma'am, frankly it is none of my business how you run your schoolroom, but I'm afraid you'll have to close the school for the foreseeable future."

"And why do you think I will I be closing *my* school?" I shot back with more vitriol than I should've allowed.

"Influenza. There were three confirmed cases this morning."

I didn't have a chance to process what he had said before I heard the click of his boots as he strode from the school house. I just stood there, frozen, trying to comprehend the words.

I jumped out of my skin as a slight clatter sounded. I whirled around to see that an abandoned piece of chalk had rolled off of one of the desks and onto the floor. I shook myself and collected it for whichever student would need it whenever classes resumed.

I muttered to myself, "Well, then. I suppose Frankie will have to write lines once this thing passes."

I grabbed my books and stormed out of the classroom.

Two

nfluenza, **I thought to myself,** a flurry of images rushing through my head.

One scene won the battle for my attention.

I would have been only eight at the time. I could still remember listening to my mother's quiet sobs through the door to her bedroom after she had received a notice that her baby sister had been claimed by an influenza epidemic.

"*Papa, why is Mama crying?*" *the little girl nuzzled closer to him, enjoying the comfort of his arms while he rocked her in the old rocking chair.*

"*Do you remember your Aunt Clara?*"

She nodded, remembering how Aunt Clara always made the yummiest candies when the family would all gather for Christmas. She was excited to see Aunt Clara again.

"*Your Aunt Clara got sick, sugarplum.*" *The man pushed his glasses back into place as he said the words.*

"*We should pray for her, Papa!*" *the little girl suggested, her voice as bubbly as ever.*

He shook his head, and the little girl watched her papa in confusion. The pastor had talked on Sunday about how God always wanted His people to pray to Him when they needed help, and her aunt definitely needed help to feel better.

"*Sugarplum, your Aunt Clara, she's—*" *he paused, trying to decide how to make his baby girl understand.* "*God decided to bring her home to Him to be one of His angels.*"

She nodded, seeming to accept what her Papa had told her. He breathed a sigh of relief that she had accepted the news well.

She sat up as something occurred to her, throwing one of her braids over her shoulder as she did so, "But God won't need her at Christmastime, right? She can still make us candies, right, Papa?"

He let out a slow exhale and brought the little girl close to him, silently praying God would give him the words he should say to his precious daughter.

I stumbled as my boot caught on a tree root, pulling me back into reality. Somehow, I'd already gone the distance from the schoolyard to the heart of town while in the haze of memory. How I longed to be as unable to comprehend reality as when I was a little girl. I didn't even want to take in the fraction of understanding the doctor's statement had given me.

Maybe the doctor could have made another mistake. It could be that he hadn't properly diagnosed his patients, right? I knew it probably wasn't the case but still didn't want to believe anything to the contrary.

Mrs. Larson paused her sweeping outside the mercantile to wave cheerily at me. I tried to match her enthusiasm as I returned her wave. Inwardly, I was grateful for the distance separating us so she wouldn't try to talk to me. I didn't know if I could handle a conversation without falling apart.

A group of eight of my students were playing ball in the street, and they called out to me as I passed. Their excited play should have made me feel some semblance of happiness, but instead it filled me with a bit of horror as I realized that I may never see these children healthy again.

I knew I shouldn't terrify them, not that they would really understand to begin with, so I waved back as energetically as I could manage.

"See you tomorrow, Miss Miller," one of the students called.

I didn't have the heart to correct her, so I just smiled and, as soon as I could without seeming rude, I quickened my pace.

The young sheriff gave me a nod as I walked past the jail. His expression was more subdued than usual. *At least I'm not the only one with this burden*, I reassured myself. I nodded back and offered a tense smile.

How would the rest of the town learn? It seemed the *doctor* had told a few people in town; what was he waiting for to inform the rest? Was he planning to let the news, the rumors spread by word of mouth? I certainly didn't intend to help him in his rumor-spreading.

I continued to ponder over what the next few weeks would hold as I walked away from the town and down the road that would eventually lead to the farm where my sister lived.

As I walked, I observed the trees blowing in the chilly wind. Most of them had long since lost their leaves, but a few stubbornly kept their hold on the last remaining few brown adornments.

Maybe it will have passed by Christmas. It has to, right? I needed to believe everything would be back to normal by Christmas. I'd *just* discussed plans with the reverend for the hymns I'd need to prepare for the Christmas service. He'd even included a new favorite, *Away in a Manger*. I wouldn't be able to bear it if we missed the Christmas service.

At long last, I'd reached my sister's farm.

The door creaked as I pushed it open and entered the house I shared with my sister.

"Anna, I'm home!" I called.

She emerged from under the table, laughing as she pulled my nephew after her and sat him on her hip as she stood. Her golden hair that had tumbled loose from its pins, further radiating her happy glow. "How was your day?"

"Well, *Doctor Williams* came by my classroom after school today," I said, contempt dripping from my voice as I set down my books and sank into a chair.

A little too excitedly, she sat down across from me at the table and leaned forward, interest etched on every part of her face. "Oh? What did he want?" she sounded a little too excited.

"He *informed* me that school would be cancelled next week due to an influenza epidemic."

I watched as her expression turned from teasing to pensive as she processed my statement. It was then that I realized that I'd spread the news about the epidemic *some* for the doctor, but it doesn't count as spreading rumors if you're talking to your sister anyway.

"No," she breathed, her brightness dimming a bit as she took in the news.

"That's what he said."

"God protect us and everyone else in the town," she whispered. "Only He knows how much we'll need Him in the next few weeks."

Three

A**nna passed me another ball** of light gold-colored cookie dough.

Normally, I avoided baking like it was... well, influenza, but for Christmas cookies, I'd sacrifice – even if they were sugar cookies. She was doing the worst part – balling up the dough – anyway. I took the ball of dough from her and rolled it in my bowl of sugar, ensuring it was coated completely. After placing the ball on the baking sheet, I held out my hand for the next one.

Normally baking Christmas cookies was solely Anna's responsibility as I was teaching during the day and she enjoyed baking, but since I was going to be home with her for the foreseeable future, I could not escape the activity.

She plopped the dough into my hand right as a knock sounded at the door.

We exchanged a look. The probability of a neighbor knocking on the door in these circumstances was incredibly slim, unless they were truly desperate for help.

"I'll get it!" we both said at the exact same time.

"My hands are cleaner," I said, as I brushed the excess sugar from my hands onto my skirt.

She grinned and said, "I'm closer!" Then she ran toward the door.

Unceremoniously, I plopped the ball of dough back into her bowl and charged after her.

She won.

I tried to compose my features and look somewhat presentable as she opened the door.

"May I help you?" she asked whomever was on the other side of the door, her tone prim and proper as can be.

"Good morning, Mrs. Parker, is Miss Miller available? I would like to speak with her," the unmistakable voice said.

Please say no, please say no.

"Absolutely, she's right here," Anna opened the door wider, revealing me standing just behind her.

Surely, the sheriff would understand if I committed sororicide.

Anna gave me a *look*.

I gave her the *look* right back, wordlessly promising revenge.

If Anna expected me to invite *that* man into the house, she could just keep right on waiting.

Most might have missed her steadying intake of breath, but we'd been sisters far too long for it to go unnoticed. "Would you like to come in?" she asked, undoubtedly trying to cover for my rudeness.

"I've just been around some of the patients who have the influenza, ma'am, and I would hate to bring it to your baby," he said. "Would it be possible for me to speak to Miss Miller outside?"

"Yes, Lydia would be happy to speak with you." Her words sounded polite, but I'd been her sister long enough to feel the bite directed my way.

She stepped back, waiting for me to pass. It would appear I had no choice but to engage in *another* conversation with the incompetent excuse for a doctor.

I stepped onto the porch, closing the door behind me. I didn't plan to be civil, and I didn't need any more of a lecture when I went back inside the house.

He stood there, looking more worn than the last time I'd seen him. The barest trace of rings could just be detected under his blue eyes, and his hair was slightly out of place.

Too upset to take any real concern at his appearance, I decided to get the exchange over with. "What do you want?" I flung at him.

"Miss Miller, I was hoping to ask a favor, and I would be willing to pay, of course." He seemed almost nervous. *Good*, he should be.

"What?"

"A lot of people have the influenza in town."

"I'm aware."

"I cannot manage it all on my own," his voice sounded a bit pained, as though he was reluctant to admit what I already knew — he couldn't handle his job.

I guessed I'd just spell it out for him. "And you expect me to be surprised by your incompetence because?"

"I could use the assistance of a nurse."

"Okay? See if the mayor will hire one."

"I was hoping you would agree to be that nurse."

"*Me?*" I paused, stunned. Bewildered. "Absolutely not. I'm a *teacher*."

"The school won't be open until this epidemic passes, and then you could go back to teaching."

"I don't have *any* medical training." Or tolerance for the insufferable man's presence.

"I've seen you; you have a great capacity for kindness and don't lose your head in stressful situations. I'll help you learn the rest." I could see the pleading in his blue eyes, but I ignored it, refusing to give in to him.

"I can't get my nephew sick, and I refuse to lose my sister, either," I said firmly. "They have already lost enough."

"I had a plan for that if you'd be willing to—"

"Why don't I make it more clear to you?" I was long past attempting to be polite. "I will never *ever* work for the man who murdered one of my students. Ever. There is nothing you can say to convince me, even if I felt like there was a sliver of a chance I would be able to do the job without endangering myself and everyone else I love!"

I didn't give him a chance to respond and ignored the twinge of guilt at the glimpse of his fallen expression as I slammed the door behind me as I went back into the house.

Anna stood right inside the door, ready to accost me.

"What was *that* all about?" she accused.

So much for the door providing any sound barrier.

"You know *exactly* why I won't help him," I shot back.

"What, because you're more stubborn than a mule and as forgiving as the average rabid badger?"

I ignored that. "You know what he did."

"Lydia." She paused, as I reluctantly met her steely gaze. "He didn't save my *husband*, either."

"Exactly! He's incompetent and arrogant and the whole town *still* thinks he is some sort of a hero."

"Or maybe God just calls our loved ones home before we are ready." I could just see her eyes begin to turn glassy as she said the words, as she recalled losing her husband just over a year before. Her expression changed as she hurled the next words at me, "And last I recall, there was a time where you were even *interested* in Doctor Williams."

"A tall man with dark hair and deep blue eyes can still be a murderer."

"Lydia!"

"It's true!" I put in, eager to get the last word. "Now, can we go back to making cookies?

Four

S**omehow, three days after** the announcement of the influenza spreading through town, I found myself in a wagon with my older sister and nephew heading to drop off a load of the cookies we'd made the day before to a widow who owned a ranch just outside of town.

"Anna, I know you've got a sweet heart and all that, but are you *positive* it is a good idea to be delivering baked goods at a time like this? You cannot afford to let yourself or little Josiah get sick!"

"You're making it sound like I'm headed for the sick ward at the hospital, Lydia!" she said, exasperation coloring her voice. "I'm just going to leave a batch of cookies on a neighbor's porch; there's as great of a likelihood of me contracting the influenza by sitting stuck at home in my front parlor as there is in going to an old woman's front door!"

"And you couldn't have chosen a neighbor who lives a bit closer to town?"

"The fresh air will do us all a load of good, and even you could tell how fussy Josiah was getting from being cooped up in the house all day."

"There's also fresh air by the clothesline at home."

"You did agree to come, Lydia."

"*Somebody* needed to watch little Josiah."

The angel in question took the exact opportunity to coo in my arms as if agreeing with me. There was a reason I loved him so much.

My sister shot me a look as she pulled the wagon to a stop in front of the large ranch house.

Mrs. Davis was riding toward us on her favorite stallion. Something about how she looked riding that horse seemed a bit... off, but before I could put my finger on exactly what it was, she tilted to one side and fell off the horse in a horrifying slump.

I leapt from the wagon and sprinted toward her still form, my skirts swishing around me as I ran.

I knelt beside her, looking for injuries as I spoke, "Mrs. Davis, can you hear me?"

No sign of acknowledgement was apparent on her face, which was surprisingly damp in spite of the slightly chilly day.

I continued talking to her as I looked for injuries. Her left wrist was at an odd angle, but otherwise, I could distinguish no visible injuries. Even more than the broken wrist, I was most concerned that she wouldn't rouse. My concerns were only heightened by my suspicions that she had contracted the influenza.

I looked up at the sound of galloping hooves. A cowboy I didn't recognize was riding towards us. He reined in his horse and dismounted.

"We told her to leave the ranching to the rest of us with her in her current state," he said. "In this instance, I don't think I appreciate being right. What happened, Miss?"

"We were just pulling in, and we saw her tumble off her horse. She won't awaken, and it seems her left wrist is broken."

He nodded and looked behind me. "Ma'am, don't let the child come near. Mrs. Davis has the grippe."

I turned around and saw my sister, who was currently balancing Josiah on her hip, nod and take a step backward instinctually.

"Would one of you ladies be willing to take Mrs. Davis' horse and fetch the doc while I get her into the house?" the cowboy asked.

I looked at Anna pleadingly, hoping she'd somehow be willing to fetch the doctor.

She just shook her head, that shadow of terror I'd come to see too often crossing her face at the thought of having to ride a horse.

Since the cowboy was here, I didn't say it out loud, but I shot her a look that should indicate the exact size of a pile of Christmas cookies she would owe me for making me go beg help from a man she *knew* I despised.

"I'll do it," I said reluctantly, as I rose from the ground and dusted off my hands. I couldn't help but wonder how much of the silent exchange the cowboy had decoded.

The cowboy fetched the stallion from where it had been grazing and led it to where I was standing. Looking up at the animal, I realized the horse was much taller than I'd thought.

How did Mrs. Davis even get on *that animal?* Desperate not to show any sign of discomfort around horses in front of my sister, I reached for the pommel of the saddle and fit my foot in a stirrup.

"May I?" the cowboy asked.

I nodded, and he gave me a boost up into the saddle.

I adjusted my seat and grasped the reins. "I'll be back as soon as possible," I said and rode off to town, dreading the upcoming interaction with the last person I wanted to be begging help from.

Five

I t'd been a good while since I'd ridden a horse, but fortunately this stallion —I'd forgotten to ask what his name was—was easy to ride. He seemed to understand instinctively what I wanted as we set out at a brisk pace toward the town.

I'd forgotten how much I enjoyed riding, or maybe the stallion was just exceptionally easy to ride. I marveled at the creature's beauty as the sun made his chestnut coat glisten, and his black mane caught the wind.

My thoughts turned to the upcoming mortifying task: asking a man for help—the *doctor*, no less—*especially* since I had turned down his request for aid only a few short days ago. Maybe his memory would prove as faulty as his medical skills.

One could only hope. I was not prepared for whatever he would say when he found me begging for help!

Unexpectedly, the horse started turning to the right. I was about to correct him when I realized that the horse was actually going the right way. My concentration could've been better apparently. I was the one chosen to go find medical assistance, and I couldn't even remember where I was going better than a *horse*.

For the next turn, I ensured I was the one nudging the horse the way he needed to go, but I could tell the horse already knew where to go if I was being honest. Well clearly, *it* didn't have an influenza epidemic, incompetent doctors, or other grievances to worry about.

I tried not to acknowledge the pit that formed in my midsection as I saw the deserted main street of town. The town was hardly bustling at its busiest times, but usually people would mill about, talking and laughing as they entered or exited the mercantile or waited for their turn at the barber shop. Even though businesses were festively decorated for the holidays, the whole place still felt empty.

Now, besides me and my horse, there was just a horse tied to a post at the mercantile. The only sound was from the breeze that blew bits of fallen garland through the street.

The door to the mercantile opened and the doctor himself stepped out onto the porch.

I drew in a breath to give myself courage and nudged the horse forward.

He looked my direction.

He looked... exhausted. His normally pristine dark hair was out of place. Dark stubble lined his jaw. Even deeper circles wound their way around his blue eyes than the last time I'd seen him.

I prodded the horse a few steps forward. so I didn't have to yell my news for whatever was left of the town to hear.

"Mrs. Davis fell off her horse. She also has the influenza. I hope at least some of that is within your skillset."

He didn't rise to the taunt, only mounted his bay horse in one fluid motion belying his exhaustion. I turned mine around and set off toward the ranch at a brisk pace after ensuring I heard the clopping sound of his horse's hooves following me.

We hadn't even gotten to the end of Main Street before he caught up to me and tried to engage in conversation.

"Tell me *exactly* what happened."

"I told you; she fell off her horse. She has influenza."

"What happened when she fell off her horse?"

"She was riding toward us and just fell."

"What happened after she fell?"

"I went to fetch a doctor whose incompetence I'm becoming more and more aware of."

I swore I could hear him take a steadying breath before continuing, "Did anythi—"

"I believe we are trying to get back to the scene of an *emergency*. I believe haste would be best, *Doc*."

"I need—"

I ignored him and pushed the horse into a gallop. Whatever his reason for badgering me, I did not need this interrogation or for him to accuse me of not doing everything I should have before running off to get what was *supposed* to be more competent help!

A few seconds later he joined me in the race back to the ranch.

I relished the feel of the air blowing in my hair as we flew forward. I'd almost forgotten how irritated I was when the infuriating man pulled in front of me.

I pushed the horse faster and took the lead again. He thought he knew better than I on everything. Well, he didn't. And he wasn't going to best me at this, either.

The doctor was probably the better rider, but the horse I had borrowed was obviously better at racing even with a less-than-experienced rider on his back. I really needed to figure out what his name was. I couldn't keep calling him "horse."

We were neck-in-neck most of the ride, but as we passed the last bend before turning into the ranch, I urged my horse to sprint ahead one last time.

I stopped a little ways in front of the house, taking a minute to relish my victory. And then I looked down.

I'd forgotten how massive the horse was.

Nausea hit me in an instant. My head felt fuzzy.

Nothing could convince me to even *attempt* to dismount, even if I thought there was a hair of a chance I could manage the feat without significant bodily injury.

Of course, the doctor took that exact moment to appear.

He had no issue dismounting from *his* horse.

He walked over to me. It would appear he'd noticed my dilemma.

"I'll be in in just a minute," I said, my voice a bit too cheery.

"Let me help you," he said.

I shook my head. "Mrs. Davis needs your help. Go ahead."

"No. I need to ensure you get down safely."

How was I going to get out of this? "Just send the cowboy out to help me. Then you can take care of Mrs. Davis faster."

His gaze hardened at the mention of a cowboy, and his voice was firm as he stated, "I'm not leaving until I know you're safely on the ground, Miss Miller."

"Doctor Williams. I won't fall off my horse. Go."

"I already have to deal with one horse-related injury. I'm not going to risk having to deal with a second."

I couldn't argue with that logic. "Fine," I huffed.

I swung my leg over the horse and felt a tingle go up my spine and had to take in a sharp inhale as I felt the warm pressure of his hands encircling my waist.

He released me as soon as my feet hit the ground.

I took a few steps as I turned away from the horse.

The world spun. I reached for the nearest thing to keep me from falling and closed my eyes as I waited for everything to stop.

"Are you feeling alright?" His voice was gentle. I didn't even bother to care.

"Mmhmm. It will pass in a moment," I said, my eyes still closed. This dizziness happened with some frequency, but did it have to come at a time when the *doctor* was audience to my weakness?

I opened my eyes a few seconds later and realized with mortification that his arm had been my anchor. He was looking at me a little too intently. I released his arm like it had burnt me.

"Does that happen often?"

"Occasionally."

"Are you feeling better now?"

I pinned him with a glare. "Mrs. Davis, remember?" and I turned and walked toward the ranch house.

Six

Mrs. Davis was sitting up in bed when we went inside. I breathed a quiet sigh of relief. If she was sitting up, her injury couldn't have been too severe.

I watched as Doctor Williams asked her questions and performed his examination. I hated having to admit that he sounded competent.

Guessing he'd need some water and bandages, I retrieved them from the kitchen. He thanked me more profusely than the simple action required.

I wanted to do more, but I could not think of any other ways I could help. I knew next to nothing about medicine, so I had to admit defeat in my mental search for usefulness.

Deciding I was probably intruding, I stepped out of the room to see where Anna and Josiah had ended up.

I found them in the parlor of the large ranch house. Biting back a comment about my concerns with the baby being in the house as someone infected with the influenza, I greeted my sister.

"Did I miss anything important while I was being forced to abide the presence of my nemesis?" I asked.

"No, not really. Mr. Shepherd—the cowboy—just got Mrs. Davis into her room and spoke with her while we waited on you and the doctor to return."

Josiah squirmed around to look at me in the confines of his mother's arms and gave me the biggest grin.

I held out my arms for him. "Since you forced me to handle Doctor Williams, I get the baby."

She rolled her eyes, but passed me my nephew, anyway.

A few minutes later, Mr. Shepherd approached our little trio. "My aunt wouldn't mind if y'all said hello, but she won't ask since she doesn't want give anyone the grippe."

I stood and passed Anna the baby. "I'll say hello."

"We'll just peek in," Anna said, rising with Josiah in tow.

She passed me the basket of cookies I'd long since forgotten. "I bet she'll need these more than ever."

As expected, Mrs. Davis was thrilled to see us. While we visited, I could practically hear her inner debate over whether to end the visit early or just enjoy the company while it was here.

The visit did not end up being extraordinarily long, but it was always nice to talk with the sweet woman.

Doctor Williams was the one who ended the visit, stating that he needed to see to his other patients. Mrs. Davis insisted that the rest of us leave with him, claiming she needed rest, but I could tell she would not have minded if we stayed.

I half-considered insisting we stay, but I realized it was getting close to Josiah's naptime, so I didn't argue.

Doctor Williams hung back to talk to me after exiting the ranch house.

Too worn out to come up with an excuse to avoid him, I let him approach me.

"I appreciated your help today," he said.

I shrugged. "I wasn't going to just do nothing," I said, even though I didn't feel like I'd actually done much of anything. "And Mrs. Davis is a sweet lady; I wasn't going to just allow her to receive subpar care."

He studied me before continuing, "Would you like to come with me tomorrow, so you could come visit her?"

Spending extra time with him sounded about as wondrous as finding coal in your stocking on Christmas morning, but I did want to see how Mrs. Davis was doing. Fortunately, one circumstance made it convenient for me to refuse spending any excess time in the man's presence: "The horse belongs to Mrs. Davis, so I am afraid I would be unable to go."

"I won't be using the buckboard tomorrow, so you two could take it!" Anna called out from up ahead, a little too cheerfully.

Doctor Williams raised an eyebrow questioningly.

I nodded my assent.

"Would tomorrow morning around ten be convenient for you?"

I nodded, regretting that I'd agreed to go with him already.

Eager to avoid any further conversation, I scrambled into my seat next to Anna in the buckboard.

"I'll see you tomorrow, ma'am," he said.

Seven

I fiddled with my loose braid while I waited. He said he'd be here at *ten*. It was closer to *eleven* at this point.

"Your hair *does* look really pretty like that, Lydia," Anna said from her spot in the rocking chair where she was knitting yet another new project.

I glared, hoping she didn't notice my cheeks burning. "I had a headache; I needed a looser hairstyle."

"And it has absolutely *nothing* to do with the fact that a handsome gentleman is taking you out for a ride later today?"

My nephew let out a squawk, so I took the opportunity to cross the room and pick him up to avoid answering. She should know that I could not care less *what* the man thought of my appearance.

I balanced the little one on my hip and handed him a toy. He dropped the toy instantly and fisted my hair, tangling his fingers in the strands of previously neatly braided hair.

"Is your mommy so silly?" I cooed as I nuzzled the little boy.

He grinned at me in response and attempted to pull his hand out of my hair. I assisted in the task, then felt along my hair. While it was slightly less tidy than I would've liked, I came to the conclusion that my hairdo still fell in the presentable category.

I heard a knock at the door. Helpful as ever, my sister asked me to get the door. Still holding the baby, I moved to comply.

The doctor stood on the other side of the door and gave the baby a huge grin as soon as he saw him.

Which was not adorable. At all.

"Hello," I said. Anna should be happy; I was being polite.

"Good morning, Miss Miller," he responded. "It'll just take me a few minutes to get the wagon ready. Is that all right?"

My nephew grabbed my braid again, yanking it toward him. I attempted to conceal my wince as the hair pulled in the tiny boy's grasp.

I looked over to see the doctor smiling at the baby's antics.

"Of course," I said, more thankful than I wanted to admit for the extra minutes to fix my now-unpresentable braid. Apparently, the braid was not the best idea ever for today. I closed the door and plopped the baby in my sister's lap.

She grinned at me. "That was quite gentlemanly of him."

"*You'd* think so," I shot back and hurried to fix my braid before it fell out completely.

A few minutes later, I met him outside as he pulled the wagon in front of the door. I climbed up into the buckboard beside him. While it was only slightly chilly, I clutched my shawl tightly around me, telling myself I was using it for warmth, not as a shield.

"Are you ready?" he asked.

I nodded stiffly, and we were off.

It probably wasn't very polite of me, but I didn't bother making conversation as we rode. I was only suffering his company so I could visit Mrs. Davis.

He'd be more likely to take you again if you were a bit nicer to him. The tiny bit of reason niggled at me, but I refused to listen. I could be nicer to him on the way back if I were so inclined.

He was the first to break the silence. "I'm sorry I was late."

"Busy morning?" I replied.

"You could say that."

I was curious enough to hear what was going on to ask. "Do you want to talk about it?" I didn't care how he was doing, but if he had any valuable information on my students, I'd take what I could get.

"Once this is all over, we won't have the same town we used to know," was all he said.

"Is it that bad?"

He nodded. "Mr. Larson passed this morning."

Mr. Larson? I thought. The owner of the mercantile always seemed to be healthy every time I'd seen him. I would hardly say I knew him well, but I remembered how he would always have a special trinket to give my nephew when we visited the mercantile.

"Has there been anyone else?" I asked. Then worried he would think we hadn't cared to inquire after our neighbors, I added, "We don't get much news, and we've tried to avoid being around people, so Josiah won't get sick."

He rattled off a list of names, some I recognized, some I didn't. Apparently being a teacher did not mean you knew everyone in town. I tried to veil my reactions as he listed off too long of a list of names. Too many of the names were people I'd known. Our town wasn't even large, and we'd already had that many people *die?*

I was going to try to formulate some kind of response, but he'd just stopped the wagon in Mrs. Davis' yard. Mr. Shepherd, the cowboy from before, stepped out the front door and came to greet us.

"Mornin'," he called.

Doctor Williams jumped out of the wagon and secured the horses while I took a much longer time untangling myself from the seat. I'd wanted to be out of the wagon long before he could finish with the horses to avoid him offering to help me down.

Fortunately, Mr. Shepherd came over and offered me a hand down instead.

"How is Mrs. Davis doing?" I asked, hoping that she had recovered significantly since yesterday.

Mr. Shepherd hesitated a bit long before answering, "She'll be excited to see you."

Well, at least she's coherent enough for him to expect her to be glad to see me. Or at least, that was the best I could come up with to comfort myself. That list of names the doctor rattled off was long enough as it was.

I stepped into the large ranch house, trying not to let my nervousness show. It wasn't even like I had good cause to be uneasy, I just didn't know what to expect. Of course, I wanted to know how Mrs. Davis was doing, but other than just checking in on her, I did not know what I was supposed to do. *How long is this visit going to last anyway?*

While I was busy worrying away, Mr. Shepherd had opened the door for us and now was discussing his aunt's status with Doctor Williams. I pursed my lips as I realized that Mr. Shepherd was the only one here to take care of her. *Wouldn't it be better if she had a woman to help her with her more personal needs?* I tried to shove the concern aside. Surely, it wasn't my place to be worried about that.

"Would we be able to go say hello?" Doctor Williams asked.

"'Course," the cowboy replied.

Mr. Shepherd led the way, and I followed. Doctor Williams trailed a bit behind me. I wondered why he let me go ahead of him. Supposedly, Mrs. Davis needed to see the doctor more than she needed to see me. If it was anyone else, I might've assumed it was chivalry, but I knew better than to expect that from the good doctor.

It was only a quick turn down a warmly lit hallway, and Mr. Shepherd was knocking at Mrs. Davis' bedroom door.

"I brought you some visitors," he called through the door before opening it.

Mrs. Davis set aside her Bible and a smile full of joy spread across her face as she greeted us. She was sitting propped up with pillows in her bed, sunlight from the open window matching her cheery, if a bit weary expression.

"Lydia, Andrew, how good to see you!" she beamed at us. "How have y'all been doing today?"

I didn't think I'd ever heard anyone refer to Doctor Williams by his Christian name. Not sure if I was supposed to answer or let Doctor Williams answer, I waited.

"We've been doing just fine, ma'am," Doctor Williams responded, in a warm tone

I'd never heard before. "And how are you doing this morning?"

"I am more than ready to get out of this bed. Would you mind informing my nephew?"

Doctor Williams chuckled. "Unfortunately, ma'am, I agree with him. Maybe I can take a look at you and see how soon we could get you some fresh air. How does that sound?"

"I suppose," she responded somewhat grudgingly. "Lydia, dear, come sit by me. You know how I detest getting examined by physicians."

Actually, I hadn't since it had never come up in our previous chats we'd always have whenever we ran into each other at church or at the mercantile, but I sat by her anyway. "Are you positive you are feeling alright?"

"Of course, dear," she answered. "But that's enough about me. How is that sweet nephew of yours doing?"

After a nice visit with Mrs. Davis, I found myself being helped back into the wagon by the doctor. I made sure to touch his hand for as short of a time as necessary, and I told myself I hated how his firm grip felt on my fingers.

I'd enjoyed getting to see Mrs. Davis, and while she definitely *was* sick, I let myself hope the dear woman would soon make a full recovery. But I couldn't escape the fact that I owed being able to visit the dear woman to the doctor himself. Inwardly, I groaned as I knew what I'd have to do.

"Thank you for taking me," I said as he settled onto the bench next to me, hoping that my words sounded sincere. I *was* grateful that he took me along, but I was still reluctant to *admit* it.

"You're welcome."

He did not immediately urge the horses to go, which left me wondering what was going through his head.

He turned toward me, and if he were anyone else, I would've said he looked almost nervous as he began speaking. "I was planning to drop by the Taylor's house after I dropped you off at your place, but I was wondering if you would like to see the children, too."

"Of course," I said, before realized I'd just agreed to spend even *more* time with the person I'd sworn to hate forever. "They're sick, too?"

"Most of the family."

"Who—?"

"Mr. Taylor, Frankie, Lizzie, and Simeon."

"What about Mrs. Taylor?"

"So far, she has not contracted the disease."

"Are... are they going to be okay?"

"I'm hoping they made improvements overnight," he said, but his voice didn't sound like he meant it.

Whatever his assumptions, they were poor enough he did not seem to think I could handle them. I chafed at how he concealed what he was really thinking from me, even as I realized that it really was not my place to know their prognosis. I still wanted to know. I loved my students and refused to watch any of them —I couldn't even finish the thought.

Eight

ven though I had not been here quite so often to talk to Mr. and Mrs. Taylor about Frankie's latest antics, I would have noticed that their barnyard looked different. Hens roamed freely, apparently having escaped the confines of their coop. The barn door swayed listlessly in the breeze. Aside from the clucking of chickens and creaking of the barn door, all was quiet, completely different from the normal happy scene of children tumbling about rowdily.

I was tempted to say something to Doctor Williams about it but decided I had already had the misfortune of speaking to him enough for one day. I silently resolved to at least secure the barn door before we left.

The doctor stopped the wagon and leaped out. I tried to untangle my skirts quickly enough to avoid him helping me down, but I was unsuccessful and was forced to accept his help.

Wordlessly, we walked to the door, and he knocked. I hung back, unsure of what exactly to do.

A few minutes passed before Mrs. Taylor pulled open the door. Relief flooded across her face as she saw the doctor. Wisps of hair fell around her face. Large bags under her eyes indicated she hadn't slept much. Overall, she was the picture of exhaustion

"Thank you so much for coming." I guessed she was trying to make her voice sound enthusiastic, but her weariness stole any bit of cheer. "Would you like some—"

I couldn't stop myself. "No, we're fine. Go sit down. We'll take care of things; you just rest."

After I ensured Mrs. Taylor had followed instructions and was resting in her rocking chair, I turned to face Doctor Williams. He did not clear his face of his smirk fast enough, so I pinned him with a glare.

He composed his features.

I let up on my glaring.

"Would you like to say hello to the children while I check on Mr. Taylor?" he asked.

I nodded, refusing to give him the satisfaction of me acquiescing verbally.

He indicated a doorway, and I tentatively stepped through.

Everything was quiet in the room. The three children were huddled in a bed under a mound of blankets. The two younger children were still asleep, but Frankie lifted his head when he heard me enter.

I almost wished he'd stayed asleep. Now that I was here, seeing my students, I had no idea what to do, what to say. *Why had the doctor even suggested I come here in the first place?* Why had *I* wanted to come here in the first place?

Oh, I was worried about my students.

Frankie's face lit up when he recognized me. Which meant I could not just flee the scene.

"Hi, Frankie," I said, probably a bit too hesitantly.

"Hiya, Miss Miller. What are you doing here?" he asked, then started into a coughing fit.

I rushed over to help him sit up until it passed.

"I just was hoping to see how my favorite students were doing," I replied as I rubbed his back.

"We're doin' okay, ma'am."

Obviously. "Well, either way, is there anything I can help you with right now?"

He considered for a few seconds. "Lizzie and Simeon would like a story."

Which had nothing to do with his own love for stories, I was sure, especially considering that his siblings were still asleep.

I examined the room and saw a book lying on the bedside table. It was one of my favorites, *A Christmas Carol*.

"Do you think they'd mind a ghost story?" I whispered.

He shook his head, and I set to reading.

There wasn't a chair in the room, so I walked around the room as I read. I didn't mind the excuse to put a little more energy in my storytelling, making all the facial expressions and gestures to adequately display the odious nature of Ebenezer Scrooge.

I wasn't exactly sure when Frankie's younger siblings woke up, but before I knew it, they were also listening with rapture.

Finally, we got to one of my favorite scenes, the conversation between Scrooge and his good-natured nephew. I delighted in choosing a voice for each and hoped I'd be able to recreate the voices later on in the story.

I relished reading the nephew's speech defending the value of the Christmas season.

And then I got to what I always thought was the funniest part of the scene. "*Why give it as a reason for not coming now?*" I read.

"Good afternoon," said the doctor from the doorway. I hadn't even sensed his presence.

"*... said Scrooge,*" I continued. "*I want nothing from you; I ask nothing of you; why cannot we be friends?*"

The children looked bewildered as they observed the exchange, but I figured they would figure it out soon enough. If Doctor Williams remembered enough of the passage, that is.

"Good afternoon." Doctor Williams added an extra gruff tone to his voice when he said the words.

"*I am sorry, with all my heart, to find you so resolute. We have never had any quarrel, to which I have been a party. But I have made the trial in homage to Christmas, and I'll keep my Christmas humour to the last. So a Merry Christmas, uncle!*"

"Good afternoon." This time he didn't manage to get the gruff tone quite right as he was near a fit of laughter, right along with the children.

"*And a Happy New Year!*" I continued.

"Good afternoon," he finished.

Having finished the exchange of dialogue from the book, and trying not to let my *own* amusement show, I set the book back on the table where I'd found it.

I faced the children, leaning forward and lowering my voice conspiratorially, "So which of you wants to be examined by Doctor Scrooge first?"

The trio became noticeably less enthusiastic and each looked at each other. I could sense the unspoken sibling dialogue as each tried to prod one of the others to volunteer.

"Y'all," I drawled. "He can't be *quite* that bad."

The things I had to do for these kids. They'd better know how much I loved them. My sister could *never* know about this.

Frankie's little sister, Lizzie, waved me toward her, looking like the little boost of energy from the story was depleting fast. I moved closer to her and leaned in so she could whisper to me.

"His medicine is *disgusting*," she said in a hushed voice.

I chuckled. "Would you say that about your mama's cooking?"

She shook her head quickly, indicating that would be unthinkable.

"Then why would you say it about Doctor Williams' special medicine? You know he's really proud of it, and we wouldn't want to make him sad, would we?"

She shook her head, resignation crossing her features.

"Why don't I find you another cup so you can wash down the taste of the medicine?"

Again, she shook her head.

I titled my head, silently asking why.

I could barely hear her answer: "Stay with me." She reached out her hand as she said the words.

I grasped her hand and continued holding it throughout the doctor's visit, even after the little girl fell back asleep.

Before ducking out of the room, Doctor Williams informed me, "I'm going to go talk to Mrs. Taylor."

I nodded, content to stay with the children a little while longer.

Mr. Scrooge had just made it home and was starting to feel paranoid when the doctor reentered the room.

I took note of the page number and closed the book.

"'Twould seem Doctor Scrooge here is going to spoil our fun," I announced. "He's probably going to say it's time for us to go."

The children all turned to look at poor Doctor Williams. He sighed and hung his head in an exaggerated show of contrition.

The children laughed at his theatrics.

Simeon, the smallest piped up, "Miss Miller, you are coming back tomorrow, right?"

His siblings looked pleadingly at me, silently asking the same question.

Saying no would've been like telling them they were getting no presents for Christmas, so I agreed. Why did children have to be so persuasive, anyway?

When I walked out to the wagon with Doctor Williams, I noticed the barn yard was in considerably better order than last I looked. The chickens were clucking happily in their coop as they pecked at what I assumed was their feed on the ground. The barn door was secured. Overall, everything looked a little more peaceful.

So the doctor hadn't *just* been speaking to Mrs. Taylor, after all. I did my best not to conceptualize his actions as kindness, since kind was the last word I would ever use to describe Doctor Andrew Williams.

Nine

Anna was there **lying in wait** when I opened the door. I knew to expect it, but I still would have liked a bit more time to plan a response before being barraged by her questions.

"Tell me *everything*," she demanded.

I let out a long, drawn-out sigh as I unwrapped myself from my shawl.

Josiah paused his crawling around the kitchen to grin up at me. I couldn't resist. I scooped him up and gave him a hug.

Of course, a minute later he started squirming, wanting freedom, but I still relished the moment he let me hold him.

"You're avoiding the question," Anna accused.

"No, I'm greeting my sweet nephew."

"Ly-di-uh, I need *details*," Anna whined dramatically.

"I had a nice visit with Mrs. Davis. She asked about you and Josiah. The Taylors have the influenza. The kids coerced me into reading to them."

"Wait, you went to the *Taylor's* house, too?"

"Yes?"

"So... I suppose Doctor Williams' company couldn't have been *too* terrible if you endured a *second* house call with him."

I glared at her.

She laughed.

I glared some more.

A devilish grin spread across her face. "*And*, the sight of him was *soooo* horrendous that you're *also* going to accompany him on his rounds tomorrow."

"How did you—" I sputtered.

"Lucky guess," she grinned, triumph written all over her face.

Sisters. Why did they have to exist, again?

Ten

The next morning woke me with its blustery chill. It was one of those days where the world seemed determined to let you know it was wintertime, and you would not escape the cold, no matter how hard you tried.

It wasn't quite freezing outside as I didn't have to deal with any ice or frozen puddles, but it certainly felt like it. For all of the layers I wore and even the shawl I'd tied around my head, I still shivered as I trudged to the barn.

Normally, Anna handled most of the chores on the farm since I taught most days, but Josiah had been fussy that morning, so I volunteered.

Fortunately for my already half-frozen self, Anna did not have much to do on the farm. Her dairy cow needed milked and animals needed to be fed and watered. The farm had been bigger when Anna's husband was alive, but she could not handle all of the work by herself and ended up selling a lot of the livestock and some of the land.

I was also eager to intercept Doctor Williams before Anna had a chance to make any *comments*. If I knew anything about my sister, I knew she loved to make comments that embarrassed me half of the time, whether intentional on her part or not.

I was grateful that the walls of the barn provided a shield from the wind and thus made the interior much warmer. I shed my mittens as I looked around, deciding what to accomplish first.

Gertie, the dairy cow, was lowing grumpily, so I decided to set about milking her first. I grabbed the milk pail and stool, attempted to warm my fingers, and then got to work. I hummed Christmas carols as I completed the task, partially because I loved Christmas music and partially to calm down the grumpy bovine.

"What can I help with?" a male voice that was becoming far too familiar asked from behind me.

I whirled around. Sure enough, the doctor stood behind me, silhouetted against the light streaming in from the open barn door.

He stepped forward. "Your sister told me I would find you in here," he said, sounding apologetic.

"You can tend to the horse," I replied and silently went back to my task.

He made multiple attempts at conversation, but I ignored him. I could never predict when Anna would materialize, and I did *not* want to give her the satisfaction. Anyway, I didn't want to interact with Doctor Williams, sister or no sister.

He seemed to be finishing his chores rather quickly, while I still was laboring over milking Gertie. I wasn't trying to watch him, but I couldn't help but sneak glances when I could just to check on his progress, or at least that's what I told myself.

I finally finished milking Gertie. Before I even had a chance to react, Doctor Williams had swooped in and taken the milk pail and set it in its place by the wall of the barn. Since it was so cold outside, there was no need to store it in the cellar. I went to where he'd placed it and scooped some of the milk into a smaller, separate jug for my sister and I to use during the day.

I looked around the barn. Was there anything the man hadn't done? It was so unfair how quickly he was able to accomplish the tasks that would've taken me at least twice the amount of time.

"Is there anything else I can help with?" he asked.

I hesitated, thinking. "I believe I just need to take in this jug of milk and bring in water."

"I'll get the water," he said, leaving no room for argument.

A few minutes later, everything was finished, and we were off in the old buckboard again, the poor old mare being forced out of her warm stall to give us a ride. I knew logically her winter coat would make her warmer than I currently was, but I still felt bad for not just letting her have an easy day of rest.

We started our morning just like the previous day had gone. I enjoyed visiting with Mrs. Davis, although she seemed a bit more tired than the day before. The children enjoyed listening to Scrooge's encounter with Marley and made me promise that I'd come back the next day.

"Are you up for a few more house calls?" Doctor Williams asked me.

I shrugged. "I suppose." I enjoyed getting to visit with people, and it wasn't like there was much to do back at my sister's place. Maybe I'd even be able to help a little bit. And it had nothing to do with the fact that I was becoming used to being in the doctor's presence. Nothing at all.

After a few minutes I had to know, "Who are we visiting next?"

"His name's Jake Wilson," the doctor said. "He's an older gentleman who lives with his niece."

"Oh, you mean Eva's uncle?"

"I think that was the name I heard," he replied, uncertainty in his voice.

I nodded. I remembered my old school friend talking about living with her uncle, but I'd never met the man. She'd only spoken about him a few times, and I got the impression he was not her favorite person in the world. Now I would finally get to satisfy my curiosity. I felt a little bad for intruding on her personal life, but surely, helping a doctor with a house call was a good enough reason.

Eva and her uncle apparently didn't live too far from the Taylors. I knew Eva didn't live on a farm, but I didn't know what her family did to make money, either. She'd spoken of business associates of her father's, but she was always a little vague on details. While she was bubbly and always open to socializing, she preferred to meet away from her home.

The only thing I did know was that rumors said that the late Mr. Wilson, Eva's father, used to be a bit of a gambler. When he'd died, there was speculation that he'd succumbed to injuries after a fight at the gambling tables, but I never knew what to believe.

Either way, the Wilson's house was a small structure. It certainly could not compare with Mrs. Davis' large ranch house.

Eleven

We stepped **into the** house together. Eva Wilson greeted me with an enthusiastic hug as I walked in the door. "Lydia! It's so wonderful to see you!" she gushed. "I didn't know you were working with Doctor Williams!"

"Yes, I am. How are you doing, Eva? How is your uncle?"

"I'm just... trying to keep things together, you know? And Uncle Jake is... as cantankerous as ever."

I smiled.

"Doctor Williams," she continued. "Thank

you so much for coming."

"Of course, may we go see him?" he replied.

Eva showed us back to her uncle's room.

"Uncle Jake, the doctor is here!" she called, then turned to face us. "I'll just leave y'all to it," she said to Doctor Williams and me.

She whisked out of the room, leaving Doctor Williams and me in the room with the old man.

"I've met Doctor Williams before, but I don't believe I've had the pleasure of meeting this angel," Eva's uncle said.

"Oh, I'm Miss Lydia Miller. When there's not an influenza epidemic, I teach school," I said as I crossed to the washbasin and filled it with fresh water.

He chuckled. "Well, Miss Lydia, I'd heard of the schoolteacher, but I'd never imagined she'd be this purdy."

"Why, thank you," I responded, hoping my discomfort wasn't leaking into my voice.

A vial clanked against the table, as Doctor Williams set it on the table much more forcefully than usual.

I finished washing my hands and brought the washbasin to Doctor Williams.

"While that water is fresh, dear, would you be so good as to sponge off my back," he said with an almost wicked grin. "It's mighty warm in here, and I usually don't have such a purdy lady to take care of me."

I pasted a smile on my face and moved to grab a washrag.

Doctor Williams' eyes met mine. "Miss Miller, I'll take care of that. Would you mind helping Miss Wilson to prepare tea?" The words themselves were polite, but they held an edge to them that I'd never heard. Usually, his voice was calm and gentle, but now his voice was laced with what someone who didn't know better might have thought was barely contained rage.

Dumbfounded, I just nodded and exited the room, grateful beyond words for the escape.

When we returned to the wagon, I could

tell Doctor Williams was still fuming.

Before he started expressing his anger, I wanted to say my piece first.

"Thank you," I said. "So much."

He just nodded in response.

While he was still composed, I could sense his emotions roiling beneath the surface. I wanted to say something, to see how he was doing, but I didn't know what to say.

"I'm so sorry," he said, before I had a chance to get my thoughts in order.

"It wasn't your fault."

"I should've sensed—"

I shook my head, "It's not your fault." I accentuated each word. *Would he please quit apologizing?*

"He deserved—" he started but let the rest of his thought escape like the puff of frosty air that blew from his lips.

I could tell the words weren't enough to calm him, so I supposed I'd have to work on distracting him.

"It does make me wonder if he's made comments like that to anyone else," I suggested.

"He's sick," Andrew said. "That makes people—"

"I've heard that too, but I'm not sure that's the case here."

It seemed to be working; he was looking at me with an intense look of interest written all over his face.

"There was something Eva said at one point that makes me wonder, but you could also be right."

"Do you want me to say something to her?" he asked.

"Eva likes to keep to herself. I don't think she'd open up to you."

He nodded.

Now I felt the need to change the topic *another* time. "How many more stops do we have?"

"Just a few," he said. Then, he picked up the reins, and we set off to the next stop.

The final house we visited looked small and cozy. A fireplace cheerily blew smoke into the air. A warm glow permeated from the windows. It seemed to promise calm and warmth and seemed to perfectly encapsulate Christmas spirit. Especially since my nose was likely quite the bright shade of scarlet and my toes had long since turned numb, I couldn't wait to visit the man whose house exuded such warmth.

"Mr. Smith's wife passed yesterday, so he probably will be a bit upset," Doctor Williams informed me. "It's always hard to predict how people will react to grief, but it always has some effect."

I nodded, hoping to be able to give the man comfort. I wondered how his house could exude such peace when there was no doubt so much grief and anguish waiting just beyond the door.

Doctor Williams knocked on the door.

No one answered.

I looked at him in concern.

"He's probably resting," he responded.

I nodded. It was probably true; Doctor Williams had certainly visited this man more times than I had.

Doctor Williams knocked once more before opening the door.

"Hello, Mr. Smith. It's Doctor Williams and Miss Miller," he called as we walked into the house.

Everything was still in the small house. As I'd predicted, it was a small, one room structure, but still looked incredibly cozy and homey. The room was lit with warm candlelight. The furnishings had obviously been made with great care by the man's late wife. I'd never been in that house before, but it felt like coming home.

In an alcove at the back of the home, I saw where the old man—Mr. Smith, the doctor had said—lay in bed. He had not stirred when we entered the home.

I moved a bit closer until I could see his face.

The first thing I noticed was his eyes. The light grey eyes were fixed, unseeing, gazing up at the ceiling. The rest of his face looked perfectly serene. His mouth was frozen in the slightest smile.

I knew the truth, but I still needed to verify, "Is he—" I started.

"Yes," Doctor Williams replied.

Words cannot express the wave of emotion that washed through me at the words. Grief for a man I'd never met, relief that he had obviously passed on so peacefully, bittersweetness as he was now with his beloved wife but would never see his children again, discomfort at having discovered a dead body. The emotions all warred for dominance, but I was so... shocked that none won out.

Doctor Williams solemnly approached the body and closed the man's eyes. I thought I saw him bow his head in a quick prayer, but I couldn't be sure. He might have been doing a doctor thing, though.

After Doctor Williams stepped away, I stepped closer to the man's body and touched his hand without really knowing why. I was surprised to find it was still warm. Dead bodies weren't supposed to be warm. Why was his hand warm?

"He probably passed a few minutes before we arrived, and he'd been running a high fever," the doctor explained.

I didn't know how to respond. I didn't know what to think. Why had the home seemed so peaceful, so warm, so inviting? Its last remaining occupant had just *died*.

As I nodded, I heard a small voice in the back of my mind whisper, *He's with his wife now. He's happy.* It didn't totally dissolve my unease, but it definitely eased the burden of all my tangled emotions just a little bit.

Twelve

rolled over for what must have been the hundredth time, still uncomfortable. The image of Mr. Smith's still face resting behind my eyelids whenever I closed them. My blankets should be providing a safe haven of warmth from my thoughts and worries, but they were not doing their job adequately. I wasn't really bothered by his death, or at least I didn't think I was, but I still didn't know what to make of the whole encounter.

I decided that only one thing would help at this point; I needed food. I had barely picked at my dinner enough to deter my sister's concerns, but now I needed food. Cookies, more accurately, but I couldn't decide whether or not I should risk waking my sister for the comfort of a few gingerbread men.

Finally, I heard the blessed cry of my nephew, and I took the opportunity to leap out of bed and go find him. Seconds later, I burst into my sister's room and scooped up the little one before Anna even had the chance to sit up all the way.

Anna mumbled something incomprehensible, but I reassured her that I could take care of the baby, and he probably just needed to be changed anyways.

The baby did need a change, as I had predicted. After he'd been properly cleaned up, he looked like he had no intention of going back to sleep, so I set him on the floor on a blanket to play. Since we were both apparently going to be spending the night awake, I set about lighting a fire in the stove; I didn't want my sweet nephew getting too cold.

As I looked at the stove, my desire for cookies only increased. I needed some gingerbread cookies; it wasn't just some passing whim. Now that I'd decided that, I knew I wouldn't be able to sleep until I'd had my cookies.

My nephew looked content on the floor, so I grabbed a bowl from the shelf, retrieved the recipe card, and set to work. Fortunately, we had all of the ingredients already in the house. Hunting eggs at midnight did not sound appealing.

I stretched up on my toes, straining to reach the jar of molasses. *Why does Anna have to keep everything so far out of reach?* My fingers could just barely brush the cool glass.

A knock sounded at the door. *Who would be coming to call at* this *late of an hour?*

I let the molasses jar stay stubbornly inaccessible for a bit longer and crossed to the door.

I was already reaching to unlatch the door but remembered what my late brother-in-law had said about not letting people in if you are not expecting them if you do not even know who they are.

"Who is it?" I asked through the door.

"It's Andrew—Doctor Williams," the far-too-familiar voice responded.

I yanked open the door, trying to contain my fury. I didn't entirely know why I was suddenly so upset besides the stress of the day, or the previous day, I didn't know which. And anyway, I still hadn't forgiven him for not doing what he should have for Johnny.

"You'd better have a *very* good reason for showing up at my door *unannounced* at this late hour," I exploded at him.

At the exact same time he said, "Is everything alright? What are you doing up so late?"

I knew I hadn't minded being around him earlier that day, but that didn't give him *any* excuse to show up, unannounced, at my doorstep at who-knows-what hour of the night! I took a breath and started over. "Why are you at my house right now?" Well, at least my tone was calmer.

"I saw the lights and thought—" he paused. "Is everything alright?"

"Yes," I answered and then a loud clatter came from somewhere behind me.

He arched his brow.

"My nephew couldn't sleep, either."

"Are you *sure* everything is okay?"

I let out an exaggerated sigh, *couldn't he just leave me alone?* I was attempting to bake to make sense of my emotions and did *not* need any further distraction, much less an audience! "Would you like to come in and *verify*?"

He just looked at me.

"Are you serious?" I could not believe the audacity of the man.

"Both you and your nephew are showing unusual sleeping patterns and there is an influenza epidemic. I do not need two more patients dying on me because I didn't verify you were well."

My nephew let out a wail. "Fine, but only because I can't argue with two insufferable boys at the same time."

"I thought you were a schoolteacher," he responded.

"I can send those miscreant boys to the corner. Unfortunately, I don't think I do that with you *or* my eight-month-old nephew."

He chuckled as he followed me into the house.

I looked around, taking in the state of the room. My nephew had managed to crawl from the kitchen, leaving behind a trail of chaos as he had somehow managed to bump into the table just so to result in some cups falling off the counter, one of which had been filled with flour. The little rascal was covered in the powder and had tracked it into the sitting area where he was playing with a captured cup.

He giggled as I walked toward him and lifted him high into the air. As I set him on my hip I smiled and said, "Here's your patient; as you can see, he is feeling quite well."

"Nevertheless, I must examine him myself," he said, cooing the words to the wee one. "It is hard to tell under all that mess."

I handed the boy to him and went back to the kitchen, trying very hard to ignore how he made Josiah smile.

After sweeping up the mess of flour on the floor, I examined the ingredients I had left on the table. I tried to ascertain which part of the recipe I'd left off on. Oh, yes, the molasses. I reached for the jar again.

"Your turn, Miss Miller."

I wheeled around, surprised I hadn't noticed his approach.

"I already told you; I'm fine!"

He pointed toward the jar with his free hand. "I'll get it for you if you let me examine you."

I glared, but he didn't waver. "Fine."

He passed me the baby, who promptly nestled his head against my shoulder.

"May I see your hand?"

I gave him the most exasperated look I could muster as I held out my hand. He pressed his fingers to the inner part of my wrist for a few seconds while he continued asking his questions.

"Have you experienced soreness in your throat?"

"No."

"Coughing?"

"No."

"Headaches?"

"I already told you; I feel completely ordinary! There's nothing wrong with me!"

He gave me another of his stares. He released my wrist. "May I?"

I didn't know exactly what he was referring to, but I nodded.

My breath hitched as he gently laid his palm on my forehead and then ran his fingers under my jawline, behind my ears, down the sides of my neck. I could only breathe again once he moved his hands away.

The room suddenly felt quite warm. My nephew shifted in my grasp, reminding me I had an excuse to leave the room for a moment.

"I need to put him down. If you'll excuse me…" I said and fled the room.

Gingerly laying the baby in his cradle, I took a minute to breathe. It was then that I realized that I had been wearing my nightgown during the entire interaction. My cheeks warmed.

I knew it was probably silly, but before returning to the kitchen, I hurried to my room and threw on a dress and pinned up my hair. Just because he saw me in such a state once did not mean he ever had to again.

Josiah had resumed crying minutes after I had set him down in his cradle, so I retrieved him as I came back to the kitchen, fully dressed this time.

I half-hoped the doctor would have left by the time I had returned, but to my dismay, he was still standing in my kitchen. Well, my sister's kitchen, but I could claim it for now; she wasn't in it.

"How much molasses do you need?" he asked, wielding the jar and a spoon.

I snatched both from him. "Shouldn't you be sleeping or tending to your patients?" I asked as I scooped several spoonfuls of molasses into the bowl.

"Now that I know a midnight cookie is an option, I won't be able to sleep until I've had some."

Gritting my teeth, I slammed the jar onto the counter.

He stole it from me and replaced the lid.

After looking at the recipe for what must have been the hundredth time, I leaned over to grab the flour at the same instant as he reached up to replace the molasses on the same shelf. I tensed as I sensed his nearness behind me.

"If you insist on staying until the cookies are done, you can at least wait in the parlor." I did not like baking for a reason, and no one needed to witness my... messiness in the kitchen.

Even without turning around, I could sense his smirk, "But you'll be rid of me faster if I help."

I threw a fistful of flour at him in response.

He laughed.

Resigned, I thrust three jars of spices at him. "Here. One spoonful each."

"Thank you."

He added the spices while I wordlessly added the sugar and flour. I attempted to avoid coating the counter in even *more* powder, but in my irritation, I was not as careful as I should have been.

"Want me to stir?" he asked.

I nodded and set about cleaning off the counter, so I would have room to roll out the dough.

"It has been a while since I've baked," he commented.

"Hmm."

"My ma used to make the best Christmas cookies. My favorites were her cinnamon star cookies. I got in trouble more than once for nicking some from the special tin she would set aside for Christmas."

He paused, probably waiting for me to respond. Silence was all he would get from me.

"What is your favorite treat for Christmas?" he asked, almost tentatively.

I let out a sigh, frustrated at needing to show some semblance of politeness and break my commitment to remain silent. "Ginger cookies. Like these."

He nodded.

I took the bowl from him and emptied the contents onto the counter. "Rolling pin?"

He pulled open several cupboards before I took pity on him.

"On the counter. To your right."

He handed it to me. I worked at rolling out the dough, so we could cut it out.

Apparently restless, he fingered the cookie cutter on the counter. "Where did you get this?"

"It was a wedding gift from my brother-in-law to my sister."

He didn't respond, just did that thing where he just *looked* at me like he always did.

"They had a Christmas wedding. A peddler had come through town shortly beforehand, and my brother-in-law thought my sister would appreciate it since she loves Christmas cookies so much."

"Did she?"

"Did she what?"

"Appreciate it," he clarified.

I nodded. "When we used it last year to make cookies, she cried."

"Losing her husband must have been hard on her."

"But she's strong. Undoubtedly stronger than I'd be."

"Oh?" he asked, leaving his question open for interpretation.

I paused mid-flouring the cookie cutter as I searched for the right words. "Anna has always been the strong one. I've always been the crier. I couldn't do what she's done, keep going like she did."

"I wonder if you're stronger than you give yourself credit for." His voice was low and sincere as he said the words.

I tried to tell myself that I hated how his words made my heart soften toward him just a little bit more than it already had.

We sat on the kitchen chairs as we waited for the cookies to finish baking. Doctor Williams had scooped up my nephew at some point, and Josiah had long since fallen asleep in his arms.

The picture was too cute to ignore.

We'd been sitting there quietly, tiredly, but he broke the silence. "Earlier, you expressed reservations about helping me since you were worried about getting your family sick."

I nodded, confused. *Did he not want me to help?* "Yes, I somewhat still worry about that. I mean, I've been changing as soon as I get home, just in case, but what else can I do?"

"I actually had an idea, if you're interested?"

I didn't know if I'd approve of said idea, but I figured I could at the worst just decline. "What is this idea?"

"You could stay with Mrs. Davis. Given the number of guest rooms she has in her ranch house, she'll definitely be able to accommodate you, and you'd be nearby in case she needs anything she'd rather have a woman helping her with."

The idea actually held merit. "I'd consider it, but I don't know if she'll agree."

"I have no doubt she'd be thrilled."

I knew that, but I still thought we'd need to ask her at least.

We sat there in silence before I decided it was my turn to make a suggestion.

"I'm guessing I've only seen a fraction of your patients you have currently, is that correct?" I asked

"Yes," he asked, wariness in his tone. "Why?"

"Even just from the few days I've accompanied you on some of your house calls, I can tell you are expending a lot of time and energy traveling between houses."

He nodded, "Unfortunately, we don't have a hospital here."

"I know, but if we found a place where we could keep the patients so you had fewer trips, you would be better able to care for each of them."

He considered before responding, "There isn't a place in town big enough to keep all of those people."

"I know there isn't a place we could fit all of them, but we could at least fit the ones who are living further from town. If we brought them to a more central location, that would eliminate most of the time spent traveling between homes, and it would make it less likely that someone dies alone like Mr. Smith."

"Is there a place you have in mind?"

I smiled. "I'm sure the schoolteacher wouldn't mind if you used her classroom since she's not teaching anyway."

Thirteen

The next morning we set our plan in motion, each of us having our own special role.

Anna would go round up healthy volunteers to help turn the schoolhouse into a makeshift hospital. Josiah would accompany her to use his cuteness to guilt people into helping.

Doctor Williams and I would see the first few patients of the day, including Mrs. Davis, to ensure that I would be able to stay at her ranch house until I was finished helping battle the disease. Once we'd secured permission and seen the most pressing patients, Doctor Williams and I would head to the schoolhouse to assist as needed and supervise progress.

Once the project at the school was completed, Doctor Williams would organize groups to bring selected patients to the makeshift hospital based on their location and ability to travel.

After dropping Anna and Josiah off in town, Doctor Williams and I found ourselves at the old ranch yet again.

The doctor said he'd take care of the horses for a minute while I went in to talk to Mrs. Davis. I agreed, although I still was unsure how to ask permission to board at someone's house for who-knows-how-long without coming off as ill-bred.

Nevertheless, I found myself knocking at the dear woman's door.

"Come in," she answered, her voice sounding weaker than before.

I opened the door and saw her in her bed once again, visibly perspiring, and I could only imagine experiencing a terrible headache.

"Hello, Lydia, dear," she said, as cheerily as she could manage.

"Hello, Mrs. Davis," I returned. I decided I wouldn't lead out with my question and instead wet a cloth so I could help bathe her face.

"Thank you, dear," she said, closing her eyes as I wiped the cool rag across her forehead, apparently enjoying the momentary relief from her fever.

"You're welcome," I answered, still unsure about how to broach the subject.

She let out a weak cough, "Where's that doctor of yours?"

I wanted to protest that he wasn't mine, but I figured the stubborn woman would take that as a sign to increase her matchmaking efforts, so instead I just said, "I think he's intentionally stalling, so we could have a chance to chat for a few minutes."

Her brow arched, "Oh? Is there something you needed to talk to me about?" Her voice gained a new energy as she saw the opportunity to lend aid.

I smiled, "I suppose so. I was wondering... I was hoping, that is—"

"Dearie, you can ask me anything in the world, you know that, right?"

I nodded, slightly encouraged. "Since I've been helping Doctor Williams, I've been hoping to find a place to stay, so I'm not risking getting little Josiah sick, and I was hoping—"

She brightened, "Would you like to come stay with me? I have plenty of extra rooms in this big empty house, and Lord knows I could use some company."

I breathed a sigh of relief. "That would be perfect."

"Sweetheart, it's an answer to prayer for me."

It would seem it was a day for miracles.

After a few more visits, Doctor Williams and I arrived at the schoolhouse. When I'd mentioned our plan to Mrs. Davis, she insisted that I have her nephew, Mr. Shepherd, along with some of her other ranch hands go help us.

The help from Mrs. Davis' ranch paired with the helpers Anna had found meant that by the time Doctor Williams and I arrived, the schoolhouse was nearly ready.

I was told the men had moved the benches out to the shed behind the mercantile. My teacher's desk had been cleared off to house medical supplies. Anna and a few women from town had begun making pallets for the patients to rest on.

The only remnants of my classroom left in place were the blackboards, the teacher's desk, and the piano we used whenever the pastor was in town for church services. It was a bit sad seeing how my classroom had been transformed, but I knew it was for a good cause, so I refused to let myself sulk.

It wasn't fancy, but it might just work.

Doctor Williams had asked for volunteers to bring patients to our little hospital, and the groups had left a few minutes before.

Mr. Shepherd and the sheriff took Anna and Josiah home on their way to collect patients, leaving me all alone in the schoolhouse-turned-hospital, waiting for patients.

The piano beaconed me, and I couldn't stop myself from sitting down to play. My fingers touched the keys, and I let myself get swept away by the music.

I swayed closer to the instrument, using the extra momentum to add more dramatic dynamics to the music. The cool touch of the keys under my fingers was so comfortingly familiar; it almost made me believe that all of this had never happened. Looking at the next measure, I decided to add in an extra arpeggio to heighten the emotion of the line, keeping the momentum strong through the note being held in the melody.

It had only been a few weeks since I'd played the piano, but it felt longer. I wanted to bask in the comforting feeling of letting my emotions drain into the keys. I would've been content to sit there for the rest of the day, pouring my soul into the music.

"That's beautiful."

My fingers stumbled from the surprise as I registered the voice.

"Thank you..." I hesitated as I completed the complicated run of notes. "Doctor Williams."

I knew I should stop and greet whichever patient he had brought in, but I let my fingers play the final few cords of the carol before rising to take care of my responsibility.

The rest of the day brought a steady stream of incoming patients. I told the men where to put each patient and hoped I was doing my job correctly. I didn't exactly know how they were supposed to be arranged, but I did my best.

While the day still passed in a blur, there were a few things that I don't think I'd ever be able to wipe from my memory, no matter how hard I tried.

Mr. Shepherd brought a little girl, four years old at most, into the schoolhouse. She barely stirred when he set her on the pallet that had been arranged for her. A few minutes later, I went to check on her and make sure she was comfortable and found that she'd stopped breathing. I'd only had time to close her eyes and pull a sheet over her small body before I had to go back to directing where to place patients.

Andrew later told me that Mr. Shepherd had buried her in the churchyard, since the rest of her family was too sick to assist. I longed to go home and let my shock and horror flow out of me, but there wasn't time.

When Andrew brought in Mr. Jake Wilson with the help of the sheriff, I thought I overheard him whisper something to the sheriff about keeping a close eye on the man, but I could have been mistaken.

The memory I'd cherish the most was when the Taylor children were brought in.

Though obviously weak and exhausted, I saw that Frankie clutched the worn copy of *A Christmas Carol* to him possessively.

An unintended but welcome consequence of bringing many patients to the schoolhouse was that it allowed more people to help. Eva had accompanied her uncle and helped me to situate parents. Andrew told me that Mrs. Taylor promised to come by later with broth for the patients. The sheriff agreed to help with shifts at the schoolhouse.

I left the schoolhouse that evening feeling hopeful about the days ahead, while grief for those we'd lost still gnawed at me.

Fourteen

would've expected the days following bringing the patients to the makeshift hospital would bring a bit of relief, but instead, I felt more distressed than ever.

I probably should have been in the schoolhouse at that moment, helping the patients, but I needed a minute to breathe, to try to get my tumbling emotions under some modicum of control.

I'd ventured outside, claiming I needed a bit of fresh air and found myself meandering through the cemetery. It hadn't been that long since I'd been here, placing a wreath on little Johnny's grave, but I could see so many changes already.

There seemed to be a new mound of freshly dug dirt everywhere I looked. Familiar names graced many more crosses. The place, once a peaceful place of refuge and reflection, now seemed to hold its breath in anticipation of receiving its next occupants.

The worst part was the mounds of freshly turned dirt didn't even represent all of the losses we'd had in the past few weeks. Many had chosen for their loved ones to be buried on their family's land instead of in the church's little cemetery.

Images flashed through my mind as I read the names etched on the crosses.

Mr. Shepherd cradling the toddler's still form in his arms.

The still, peaceful face of Mr. Smith.

Mr. Larson sneaking Josiah a treat he'd hidden behind the counter at the mercantile.

Johnny's blood staining his peaceful little face while Andrew did his best to save the boy.

The woman who'd passed while holding my hand, whose name I didn't learn until after she'd died.

The infant being held protectively in her mother's arms while the mother sobbed and refused to let the child go.

Hot tears burned my wind-nipped cheeks as I let silent tears fall for the ones I'd met and the ones I'd never meet.

So much life, taken too soon. I fell to my knees, right there in the middle of the frosty ground.

What are we supposed to learn from this? I prayed. *How are we supposed to see Thy hand in all this? Sustain me, Father. Help me to have faith in Thee and Thy plan.*

A warm hand settled on my shoulder. I didn't have to look up to know it was Andrew.

"Are you alright?" he asked, worry brimming in his blue eyes.

"I will be," I responded. "Let's go inside."

He helped me to my feet, his warm hand clasped in my frozen one, and I walked with him to the schoolhouse, hand in hand.

Fifteen

The old lady looked up at me, moonlight highlighting the gentle care etched on her face. "Tell me who to pray for."

Who didn't *need prayers?* I thought for a minute and rattled off some names for her list.

"And what about you?" she asked.

"Me?" I asked. "I'm not even sick."

She smiled gently, despite the exhaustion playing on her worn face, "If we only needed prayers when we experienced illness, the good Lord would get mighty bored up there."

Her words echoed through my mind as I went to the schoolhouse hospital that morning.

Andrew met me at the entrance of the building. "How are you this morning?" he asked.

"Tired and a little cold, but I'll be okay," I returned with a slight smile. "What about you?"

"Better now that you're here," he returned with a grin.

I couldn't restrain a matching grin from spreading across my face. Or the blood that pooled in my cheeks, warming my face instantly, at the words.

I followed him inside, energized for the day ahead, even though I knew it would bring its own sorrows.

I decided to start my morning by saying hello to the Taylor children and giving my promise to read to them later in the day. Mrs. Taylor had visited the day before, and she'd told us she felt the children were improving. I hoped she was right.

The children were still asleep. I knelt next to Frankie and laid my hand on his. I noticed his breath coming in short raspy bursts, but brushed my increased worry aside even as a sinking feeling opened up in my midsection.

"Miss Miller," he gave a weak smile as he said the words I strained to hear. "You came."

I returned his smile, hoping it looked genuine. "I promised I would."

"I'm glad."

I grabbed a rag and basin that was next to his pillow, wet the rag, and used it to wipe his sweaty brow.

A few seconds of silence followed.

"Miss Miller?"

"Yes, sweetheart?"

"I-I don't think—" his statement was interrupted by coughing. "I don't think I'll be able to clean those blackboards for you."

It took me a moment to remember what he was referring to. And then his words sunk in. "Frankie, of course you'll be washing my blackboards for me," I forced a smile as I said the words, setting the rag aside.

"I'm sorry, Miss Miller." He let out another weak cough. "You were a great teacher, ma'am. I'm going to miss your stories."

"Thank you, Frankie." I blinked back tears, refusing to let him see me cry. "Why don't I read to you some more?"

He nodded and closed his eyes, drifting off to sleep as I resumed reading. My voice broke as I read, but I wouldn't stop. I'd let Frankie hear his story, but with my unoccupied hand, I held his.

I felt his hand go limp, and the book tumbled from my grip and clattered to the floor.

I shook his shoulders, willing him to rouse one last time.

"Father, please." I meant the prayer to be silent, but it escaped my lips anyway. "Please."

Nothing,

"Doctor Williams!" I shouted. He could bring Frankie back. He had to!

In seconds, Andrew was at my side, examining the boy's still form.

Andrew's eyes met mine, a look I now recognized as sorrow and resignation pooling in his gaze.

I nodded my understanding and blinked back another round of tears.

Andrew began placing a sheet over the boy's still form.

An inhuman shriek split the air, and I wheeled around to see that Mrs. Taylor had just entered the schoolhouse, presumably to check on her children.

"Oh, God no! Please, please, please no! Not my son! Not my little boy!" she said, her voice cracking with each cry.

She fell to her knees next to the boy's still form, and pulled him into her arms. Rocking him as she sobbed.

Unsure of what else to do, I put what I hoped was a steadying hand on her back, trying to wordlessly communicate that I was there for her, even as silent tears flowed down my own cheeks.

After Eva offered to take Mrs. Taylor home, I was finally free to run out of the building and have my own time to mourn. I refused to show my sorrow in front of people who deserved to grieve far more than I did, so I'd restrained myself as best as I could.

Now, I sprinted from the schoolhouse, ignoring Andrew yelling after me, heedless of the rain that had begun to fall earlier that morning.

I sprinted until I collapsed against the trunk of an oak tree, letting my sobs overtake me.

The rain pelted its fury, but I didn't care. Frankie was gone. He'd never again pull a prank during class and leave me wondering how I was to contain my laughter.

The boy who loved stories, who was intensely protective of his younger siblings. Gone. And I would never be able to tell him all the things I wish I had.

I was soaked through, but I was fine with that. It would've been worse if the weather mocked my grief rather than mirroring it.

"Lydia," Andrew's voice called from somewhere behind me.

I turned to face him. Finding him standing right behind me, I fell into his arms.

He didn't hesitate to pull me to him and return my embrace. I sank against him, resting my head against his strong chest as I sobbed.

We stood like that for several minutes, me letting my grief drain from me, him providing the strength I so desperately needed.

"Lydia," he said, his voice gentler than I'd ever heard it.

I looked up into his face that was dripping with rainwater.

"Would you allow me to take you back to the ranch?" he asked.

"B-but you n-need help h-h-here," I replied.

"I love having your assistance, Lydia, but what I really need right now is for you to get out of those wet clothes before you catch the influenza next." The intensity in his eyes said more than words ever could.

I nodded numbly. Eager to leave this place of death and despair.

Sixteen

After returning to the ranch house, I followed Andrew's instructions to change into warm clothing and find something warm to eat. I'd finally stopped crying, and I even smiled slightly as I remembered how Andrew had prayed with me before he'd left to get his own warm change of clothes.

Still, the grief left a hole in my chest that I didn't know if I'd ever be able to fill. Part of me didn't know if I wanted to.

Restless, I wandered the spacious house as I tried to calm my mind.

I found myself outside of Mrs. Davis' room. Quietly, I tapped on the door, but she didn't answer.

To be safe, I decided to look in on her anyway. I pushed the door open, and saw her resting in her bed.

Mrs. Davis turned to look at me. I tried to conceal my surprise, as I thought she'd been asleep.

"I overheard you and your doctor talking about the boy." She didn't have to specify which. "Do you want to talk about it?"

I shook my head, trying to keep up the last bits of the dam I'd just managed to build up again before it crumbled away. However, looking into her kind face, my willpower dissolved like sugar in water.

"Frankie, he's – he's... gone," my shoulders curled inwards as I shook. "And I was – I was there. And right before, before it happened, he talked to me."

Mrs. Davis motioned for me to sit on the edge of the bed and waited for me to respond. Her eyes held perfect kindness. No judgement, no hurry to fill the wordless space, just there, waiting, listening for me to be ready to share whatever was on my heart.

"And you know what that boy did?" A half sob, half chuckle burst forth. "He *apologized*. Because he wasn't going to be able to clean the blackboards after school."

She gave a little cough but made no comment.

"And it's not just little Frankie. It's the little toddler, and Mr. Smith, and Mr. Larson, and a whole lot of other people that I'm surely forgetting about right now. And on top of that it's *Christmastime*. Anna and I had *plans*. No, her husband isn't here anymore, but we were still going to make it a special Christmas for my nephew. Well, I guess at the very least it'll be a Christmas to remember, but isn't Christmas supposed to be a happy time?" The words tumbled out in a rush, and I was powerless to stop them. "A time for hope and gift-giving and spending time around people you love? And this Christmas is just turning out to be just plain *miserable*, even though this is supposed to be the happiest, most hopeful time of the year! I've lost track of the number of times I've cried myself—"

"Lydia," she said, her worn hand grasping mine. "I think you're getting Christmas all wrong. Yes, Christmas honors the greatest hope we've ever been given, but remember *why* we were given that hope, sweet girl."

I looked at her, confused.

"Yes, we *want* Christmas to be a happy time, a celebration, even, but that's not how it works. We don't have Christmas for the happy times. We have Christmas—we were given Christmas—because we need Someone to wipe away our tears."

When I didn't respond, she continued, "And sweetheart, I know you miss that little boy. I know you miss him something terrible, but you know as well as I do that he's being held in God's tender care right now. Just like you are. Just like I am. Just like all of us are."

I didn't respond for a minute; I just sat there, contemplating her words. I hadn't even noticed that my cheeks were slick with tears until she lifted a frail hand to wipe away a tear before it fell from my face. I knew I should say something to fill the silence, but all I could do was run her words through my head over and over and over again.

That evening, I fell asleep mulling over her words, small swells of peace slowly beating back the waves of sorrow as I realized that what she said was true.

Seventeen

Grief hit me like a wave the instant I woke the next morning, drowning out the remnants of peace I'd clung to the night before as memory assaulted me, and I relived my last conversation with the little boy.

I knew I should get up and get dressed, so I could help Andrew with his patients, but I couldn't stand the thought of going back to that place, reliving those memories in the same place it'd happened. Anyway, it was cold.

I wrapped myself more tightly in my blankets and told myself that Andrew could manage without me for one day, even as I knew I longed to see him.

What felt like only a few seconds later, I was awakened by knocking on the front door. I leapt from the bed, hurried to pull on something semi-presentable, and braided my hair as I ran down the stairs.

Out of breath, I pulled open the door.

Andrew stood on the other side.

"Hello," I said lamely, my cheeks flushing in embarrassment for him having to come find me.

"How are you, Lydia?" he asked, his deep blue eyes boring into mine.

"I'm... I'll... I'm fine, I suppose." *What else was I supposed to say?*

"I was worried about you," he said.

I nodded.

He stood there for a few seconds.

The air was thick with awkwardness, but at least it seemed I was not the only one affected by it. I knew I should say something, I wanted to say something, but I didn't know what to do,

I just stood there holding the door open while he stood there on the porch.

He recovered before I did. "I was hoping to check on Mrs. Davis, and, well, see how you're doing."

"Oh! Of course," it was just then that I realized that I hadn't even invited him inside. I motioned for him to come in and led the way to Mrs. Davis' room.

I knocked at her door and waited for her quiet "come in" before entering her room.

"Doctor Williams came to visit," I announced.

She gave a weak smile. "Lydia, dear, would you fetch us some tea?"

I nodded and left the two to talk, ensuring I took a bit of time making the tea, and attempting not to worry about why she didn't want me in the room while she conversed with Andrew.

After dawdling as long as I figured I could get away with without seeming obvious, I returned to her room, tea tray in hand.

They stopped their conversation abruptly when I entered, so I set the tea tray down and made an excuse about needing to finish something in the kitchen.

They accepted my excuse without question, and I fled, my worries multiplying

Andrew located me in the parlor, sipping my own cup of tea.

"Are you feeling alright?" he asked.

"Physically? I'm healthy as can be."

"And aside from physically?"

I sighed, "Last I checked, if I wasn't at least a little affected by all of the death around me, most people would consider that evidence that there is something wrong with me."

He nodded. "Is there anything I can do?" he asked, sincerity coloring his words.

Hold me. Kiss me. Protect me from all of this insanity. "No, I don't think so."

"Would you let me know if there was?" his gaze bored into mine, demanding honesty.

"Of course," I replied. It was mostly true. I would ask for anything he could reasonably help me with.

He nodded, accepting my answer.

"Will—" he paused, then resumed. "Will you be joining me at the school later today?"

I should've prepared an answer. Yes, I wanted to spend the entire day with this man, but I couldn't-wouldn't go back there. It was too painful to consider. "I-I need a day," I said.

He nodded. "I'll see you tomorrow." He grabbed his coat and walked out of the room, a slight hint of dejection in his posture as he left.

Guilt tore at me as I watched him leave, but I knew I could not go back to that schoolhouse and relive those memories. Ever.

Eighteen

"LYDIA ANNETTE MILLER!"** the unmistakable voice of my sister yelled from outside. "You get out here *this instant!*"

What on earth? I thought as I hurried to slip on my shoes and go see what was wrong. *Was Josiah sick? Had something happened on the farm? But if it was one of those things, why did she sound so furious?*

I made it outside and saw my sister standing on the porch, fuming.

"What's going on?" I asked in a panic. "Where's Josiah?"

"What is this I hear about you *refusing* to help Doctor Williams with his patients?" she hurled at me.

"I didn't refuse," I said, a bit too defensively. "I just can't stand to go back there and relive—"

"So, because *one* little boy died you abandon all the rest of them? There aren't any others you care about in that school?"

"Of course I care about them!" No one in their right mind could believe anything different.

"Then why aren't you over there?"

I took a breath to steady myself. "I *told* you. Frankie died, Anna, he *died*. I can't go back there. I can't watch—"

"Of course you can!" she hurled at me. "Last I checked that little boy had a brother and sister who are still in that school trying to get better. They're probably scared stiff since their big brother just died. If they can stand to be in that schoolhouse, so can you."

I huffed. "They don't have any other choice!"

She rolled her eyes. "And what makes you think *you* have a choice?" Her voice softened just a bit. "Rumor is God's given you a gift, and last I checked, He expects us to use the gifts He's given us."

I took another steadying breath, "I'm sure God would understand if I took one day—"

"I'm sure the man who buried his talent thought the same thing," she shot back. "Now, go get your shawl and get in the wagon. You have two minutes."

I made a show of rolling my eyes, but I still did as I was told. I hated how much her words made sense.

Back outside, I asked again, "*Now* can you tell me what you did with my nephew?"

"He's with Mr. Shepherd," she said as she climbed into her spot in the wagon.

"Mr. *Shepherd?* The cowboy?" I asked, incredulous.

"Yes? Josiah loves him," she answered.

"Oh, *Josiah* loves him," I echoed, glad I now had some bit of leverage over my bossy older sister.

I paused at the door of the schoolhouse, praying the Lord would grant me courage. Anna gestured for me to go on, and if only to evade her wrath, I pulled the door open and stepped inside.

Andrew's eyes lit up the instant he saw me. He stopped what he was doing, and came over to greet me.

"I thought you said—" he started.

"Bossy older sisters," I replied. That should be *all* the explanation he needed.

He smiled, "I knew I liked your sister."

I changed the subject. "How are the other Taylor children?"

He considered for a moment before responding, "They seem to be improving."

"And do they know?"

He nodded.

"Are they okay?"

"I doubt it." He turned to look at where they lay, and my eyes followed. Lizzie was sitting up, but she looked quite upset. Her face was red and blotchy from crying.

"I'll see if I can talk to them," I said and walked over to the two children. Lizzie looked up at me through bleary eyes. Simeon still had his head buried in his pillow.

"Hello," I said quietly.

Lizzie just looked at me.

"I've been praying for you."

Lizzie shrugged. Simeon continued ignoring my presence.

Read to them, a voice whispered in my mind. "Why don't we continue reading our story?" I suggested.

Lizzie shrugged and Simeon ignored me. At least they didn't say no. I retrieved the book from its hiding place under Lizzie's pallet and began reading.

At the end of the chapter, Lizzie stopped me. "Why do you think God took Frankie?" she asked.

Heavens. I was not qualified to answer this. A thought came through my head, and I repeated it out loud. "I don't know, sweetheart, but I do know that God loves me and you and Simeon and Frankie. And in the end, He's the one who holds us in His tender care." My words echoed Mrs. Davis', but I figured there were worse people to quote.

The little girl accepted the answer and lay down on her pallet and drifted off to sleep.

Father, please comfort them, I prayed as I set aside the book.

Nineteen

As Andrew had predicted, the two other Taylor children recovered. Lizzie's fever broke the day after her brother died, and Simeon's broke the day after that.

I breathed prayers of thanks when they recovered, but I couldn't wipe the memory from my mind when they saw their brother's grave for the first time. The children shook and cried and clung to their mother, who tried valiantly to stay strong for the little ones.

The day after the children went home, I went with Andrew to the Wilsons' home. I stood behind him as he knocked on the door.

After a few minutes, Eva called through the door, "Who is it?"

"It's Doctor Williams and Miss Miller," Andrew returned.

She opened the door and invited us inside.

We entered the house, and she directed us to sit in the kitchen.

"How are y'all doin' today?" she asked brightly.

"We're doing fine, ma'am," Andrew returned. He cleared his throat before continuing, "I regret to inform you that your uncle passed this morning."

She just looked at him for a second, not responding.

"Are-are you alright?" I asked, trying to gauge her reaction.

She nodded and then dissolved into a fit of hysterical laughter.

It was... horrible. There was no other way to describe it. She seemed crazed. I didn't know what to do, how to react, and she just kept laughing.

I looked at Andrew to see if he knew what to do, but he looked as bewildered as I did.

Tears began to roll down her cheeks, even as she continued with her horrible hysterical laughter. Unsure what else to do, I wrapped an arm around her shoulders and gave her a hug.

A few moments later, she calmed down enough to speak.

"I'm-I'm—" she doubled over as another fit of laughter hit her. "Forgive me, I must seem insane."

What was I supposed to say to that?

She finally got her laughter under control for good. "Again, I apologize, I've not been sleeping well the past few nights."

"Is there anything I can do for you?" I asked, hoping I could do *something* to help her.

She shook her head, "Other than getting him buried, I should be fine."

I nodded.

"Would you prefer he be buried in the churchyard or here on your land?" Andrew asked.

"Oh, here, definitely," she answered.

I wished I knew what was going through her head, but all I could do was send a silent prayer heavenward for her.

"Would I be able to come help at the hospital?" she asked. "I just don't have a lot to do here, and now my uncle won't be able to object..."

Andrew nodded. "Of course. We could take all the help we can get."

"Well, thank you so much for stopping by," she replied. "I will see y'all tomorrow then!"

She whisked us out the door, and I was left with more questions than I knew what to do with.

Twenty

The next morning, **Andrew** came to visit Mrs. Davis. Again, Mrs. Davis assigned me a task, so I wouldn't hear her conversation with the doctor. I decided I was through with the suspense.

"How is Mrs. Davis really doing?" I asked Andrew as we walked out to the wagon together, chilly air nipping at our faces.

He hesitated.

"Is it really that bad?" I asked. I wasn't totally surprised, but I loved the old woman, and I was not ready to let her go.

He nodded.

It was my turn to nod. It would be okay, I told myself. I would make it through it.

"Do you know when?" I asked, fearing I already knew the answer.

"It might be later today or tomorrow," he said, weariness coloring his voice.

I shook my head, not wanting to believe the words.

"And there's nothing—" I started, but paused, not wanting to pressure him. After all, God was the one who was responsible for who lived and died, not Andrew, no matter how wonderful his medical abilities were.

"I wish I could do something," he started. "But she's ready to go."

I sighed and began pacing as I voiced my frustrations, "I'm so ready for this thing to be over. I-I can't fathom how you do it, and it just seems never-ending."

He took my frozen fingers in his warm grasp and just waited for me to continue.

"How-how do you even do it? How do you keep going back, knowing, *knowing* there's nothing you can really do for them?"

"Lydia."

I looked into his deep blue eyes.

"I believe, I *know* God called me to this work, but even I have a hard time remembering what my true job is."

It was my turn to wait for him to continue.

"Everyone says that a doctor's job is to save lives, but if that were true, if my job were to save lives, I'd be a failure before I even started. That's His job; He decides who stays and who He calls home," he said, his tone impassioned as he explained. "I do the best I can with the skills and knowledge He has given me, but I'm not called to save people. I believe that He has called me-us, all of us, to love, comfort, mourn, serve. I can't do His job for Him, but I can do those four little things."

"But everyone expects us to *do* something, to save them; how do you—those expectations, and all the bad that's happened, all the people who've—" my voice trailed off before I could start again. "Even knowing what He's called you to do, it can't be easy for you to keep going."

Before answering, he pulled me into an embrace. "It hasn't been easy facing these past few weeks," he chuckled, for a reason I couldn't fathom. "But there's one thing that has made it easier to face each day, each of the hard times, each of the disappointments."

"Yes, I know, G—" I started.

He cut me off. "God knew I didn't have the faith to keep going, at least on my own. So He sent me exactly what I needed to stay strong."

What had he been sent? I couldn't recall anything that had made our work easier, lighter to bear.

"Lydia," he released my hand and titled my face upward toward his own with his warm hand. "Lydia, He sent me you."

I flushed and turned my face away. I couldn't even comprehend what he was saying. *Me?* He thought *I'd* been sent to help him face the hard days?

As Andrew had predicted, later that day, Mr. Shepherd came to the schoolhouse to inform us that his aunt had passed on.

Tears flowed, but while her death was still painful, it was good knowing that she had been ready to meet her Savior.

Andrew seemed more affected by her death than I would've expected. He had stepped outside, and I found him sitting on a fallen log, a silent tear running down his face. I debated whether to go to him, or let him have his private moment of grief.

I felt a nudge that I should go to him, so I just went and laid my hand on his shoulder.

He looked up at me and said, "She was a good woman."

I nodded and sat beside him on the log.

After a few minutes he said, "She asked me to give this to you." He handed me a folded note.

I took it and put it in my pocket; I'd look at it later. Right now, I would be there with Andrew. Mrs. Davis' last words of wisdom would keep.

Twenty-One

That evening, **I decided** to read the contents of Mrs. Davis' letter. I had been itching to read it most of the day, but I wanted to ensure that I was alone, so I could react to its contents without an audience.

Dear Lydia,

If you are reading this letter, it means that I have passed on. I had Andrew write it for me as my hands could not hold a pen steady. If the penmanship is poor, that would be Andrew's fault, not my own.

I chuckled as I read those words, remembering how Mrs. Davis had been quite proud of her penmanship.

Dear Girl, you have a beautiful heart. These past few days I have praised the Lord that He has let me see how you have grown through this unimaginable trial.

Lydia, as you know, I never had children of my own, but I always thought of you and your sister as my daughters. You will find that reflected in my will.

But I did not write to tell you about the will. I was hoping to give my dear daughter one last piece of advice, if she'll take it.

Dearie, remember how good God is. Learn to trust in His timing, even if He allows tragedy to fall on Christmas Day. He has given you such beautiful gifts. Learn to use them. Don't let them go to waste.

No matter what, choose to go on living a life filled with hope. You have such a tender heart that you are affected deeply by tragedies. This is a gift and a trial. Don't let your sorrows overtake you. Let them teach you understanding.

I miss you, Lydia.

Love,

Mrs. Davis

The postscript was scrawled in barely legible cursive that I hoped I interpreted correctly.

P.S. Doctor Williams is a good man. You two would make a lovely couple.

Tears coursed down my cheeks as I read the words again and again and again. At long last, I folded it and placed it in my Bible for safekeeping.

Needing to make sense of my emotions, coupled with the fact that the pantry was looking a little bare, I decided to bake bread to try to sort out my emotions.

As I baked, my emotions festered and left me feeling upset and angry and defeated.

The bread dough was warm and had risen over double its original size. I considered pulling over a chair for added leverage but decided I was upset enough to be able to properly slam the dough into submission. I pushed up my sleeves and punched the warm lump with all my might, putting every ounce of my frustration into the punch. The first punch is always the most satisfying, but I continued to pummel the dough.

I pummeled.

And pummeled.

And pummeled.

And pummeled.

And pummeled.

And pummeled.

And pummeled.

And pummeled.

And pummeled.

And pummeled.

The dough was long past a cratered lump of goo.

But I still slammed my fists into it over and over and over again.

The boy falling from the tree.

Frankie apologizing.

Eva's hysterical laughter.

Mrs. Davis' beautiful letter.

Tears silently sliding down Andrew's face.

Anna's torn expression when I left.

The faces of the sick twisted in pain.

The cries of the delirious.

Frantic people caring for their loved ones.

I pounded out my frustration for all of them.

I didn't realize I was sobbing until it had escalated to screaming my frustrations.

Hot tears dripped from my face.

"Why?!" I scream-sobbed. "Why are You doing this to me?"

I slammed my fist into the dough again.

"What did they do to deserve this?!"

Fist pounded dough, tipping the bowl. With nothing to concentrate my anger and grief on, I collapsed to the floor.

From the ground, I still hurled my words toward the heavens, "We've done *everything* we can do. *Everything*. What more do You want from us?! It's *Christmastime*, and we don't even have time to worship You because we're too busy dealing with this epidemic *You* started. What are we supposed to learn from this?!"

I didn't have energy to hurl much more heavenward. "I can't do this anymore. I can't. I can't. I can't," I sobbed into my arms as I let myself fully collapse into a heap on the cold floor, the bread dough long forgotten.

A knock sounded at the door. I pushed myself off the floor and rubbed at my bleary eyes. I shivered in the dark room as I stumbled to find a light. I rubbed my back as it protested my intolerable behavior of falling asleep on a wooden floor.

My hip collided with the countertop, and I was sure I was going to have a bruise in a few short hours.

The knock sounded again.

"I'm coming," I called, half yawning the words.

I groped along the countertop, finally finding the matches. I struck one and lit the lamp, but not before the fire burned a bit too close to my fingers. Maintaining enough self-composure, I shook out the flame on the lit matchstick before throwing the burnt stick of wood into a pile of flour.

I stumbled my way toward the door and pulled it open.

Andrew stood on the other side.

"I just wanted to—" he started.

I collapsed into him, the brilliant sound of tinkling glass signaling that I had lost my grip on the lantern as I did so.

A split second later, I was being cradled in his arms as he stamped out the flame.

I knew I should be embarrassed by nearly burning down the edifice, but I was too drained to care.

I clung to him tighter, needing the protection and surety of his arms.

He carried me inside and set me on the sofa. He didn't even bother to take off his hat or gloves before sitting next to me and pulling me to him.

I buried my face in his chest as I sobbed.

Silently, he held me in his arms, rubbing slow circles on my back.

I didn't know how long we sat like that.

After my breathing had slowed and I was in more control of myself, I heard him whisper into my hair, "Do you want to talk about it?"

I pushed away from him, trying to regain a bit more of my composure and dignity as I tried to work out how to answer. Finally, I settled on, "I don't know."

"I'm here if you need me," his voice was soft, gentle.

"I know," I said. Then realizing that wasn't quite the proper sentiment, "Thank you."

We sat in silence for a few minutes.

"Would you like some light?"

"I'll—" I started, rising to tend to the fire.

His warm hand on my arm stopped me. "Let me."

I watched as he efficiently built a fire in the fireplace. Strange, I hadn't noticed the chill in the air until the fire was crackling.

He turned to face me. "It's too much for you, isn't it?"

"Wait, what? No!" the words came out more forcefully than I wanted, but I could not bring myself to regret it.

"I can't let you keep—"

"Andrew."

He stopped, the look in his eyes softening even more if possible.

Oh. I'd just said his Christian name aloud for the first time.

"Andrew, it is hard, and there are days I selfishly want to quit and just stay home and tune out everything going on around me, but God has made it clear that I'm supposed to be helping you. He has called me to care for the sick and afflicted right along with you. Yes, this evening has been rough, but Andrew, He has called me to help you at this time, so He is going to give me the strength to get through it." As I said the words, I was surprised to realize that after everything that had happened, I still meant them. Yes, my main reason for saying them was to ensure Andrew continued to let me help him, but it didn't make them any less true.

I couldn't read the expression on his face, but it might have been some mix of awe, joy, bewilderment, and shock.

"And you know what else, Andrew? God has sent angels to help me get through it, and I know He will keep sending me angels to help me." Before I could regret it, I continued, "This evening He sent me you because He knew you were exactly what I needed."

Twenty-Two

barely slept a wink that night, and the morning came far too quickly. My nightgown clung to me, damp with sweat even as I shivered. I lifted my hand to my temples as I tried to massage away my pounding headache.

I longed to stay abed, but Andrew needed me. I wasn't going to let a little headache stop me from helping him.

Lydia, you know you're—

I bit back the thought. I wasn't going to allow anything to stop me from helping Andrew. It had only been the day before that he had told me that he needed me, that I'd been sent by God to help him. I wasn't going to bail on him now especially for something as trivial as waking up a bit out of sorts.

I used a wet cloth to try to freshen up a bit, and I rejoiced in the coolness of the wet cloth against my warm skin, even as I longed to climb under a mountain of blankets.

A little while later, I declared myself as presentable as I was going to get. I walked out into the chilly weather and was happy to see that Mr. Shepherd had already gotten a horse ready for me.

I was even more grateful no one was around to watch my dismal mounting performance. After more attempts than I would ever admit to, I was seated on the beast and ready to ride to town.

Luckily, the horse knew the path to the schoolhouse hospital well at this point because my head just felt foggy.

Andrew met me in the yard of the schoolhouse and came to help me dismount. I was grateful I'd remembered to wear gloves so he wouldn't be able to feel how warm my hands were. As usual, he took great care to ensure I was steady after helping me dismount, which I appreciated since I was a little dizzier than usual.

"How are you doing?" he asked me.

I plastered on a smile. "Better now that I've seen you."

He led me into the schoolhouse.

I did my best to keep up with my usual pace, but I could tell I was dragging behind. As I washed one little girl's face, I wished I could use the cloth on my own warmed skin without drawing too much attention to myself. Each time I stood up, I had to take longer than usual to steady myself against a wave of dizziness.

But I was not about to stop. Andrew needed my help.

"Miss Miller," Andrew called from a few paces away. "Would you be able to clean these instruments once you're finished?"

I nodded.

Once I'd completed the task, I moved to grab the bottle of carbolic acid from its place on the table. I collected the tray of supplies Andrew had left and moved them into a bowl to be cleaned.

I opened the carbolic acid and was instantly assaulted by the overpowering sickly-sweet smell emanating from the bottle. I tried to shake off the added wooziness that came over me.

"I think I need to sit down," I said weakly.

From a few paces away, Andrew's worried eyes met mine.

Another wave of dizziness washed over me and I collapsed.

The last thing I sensed was strong arms cradling me before I surrendered to the darkness that claimed me.

Twenty-Three

could still see it plain as day. The boy falling from the tree. The blood that flowed from his head, marking Frankie's still face, weak with sickness. The blood that stuck to my fingers as I clung to the letter those children loved me to read to them.

I became aware of a cry sounding, and I turned to scoop up my nephew. The little boy held out his hands and asked for one of Aunt Clara's special Christmas candies. I crossed the kitchen and opened a bowl and fished out a gingerbread man. The boy became fussy, so I set him on the grassy ground as I went to find feed for the chickens.

The chickens were all in an uproar about an intruder in their coop, or at least that's what they told me, but as everyone knows, you can never trust a chicken. I entered the coop to investigate their claims and was greeted by Beau, my father's hunting dog. I gave Beau a hug and informed the chickens that Beau was a friend, not an intruder.

The chickens were a bit skeptical of my assertion, but had no choice but to trust me. I took Beau to his doghouse before I entered the schoolhouse to prepare to teach my lessons.

Dear Father, I know you've been getting a lot of requests...

I entered the schoolhouse and saw an apple sitting on my desk. I picked it up and a large brown worm crawled out of it and onto my hand. I shook the worm onto the floor and saw Andrew standing in the corner of the classroom.

Funny, I couldn't remember why I'd put him in the corner. He usually didn't deserve to be in the corner.

Nevertheless, I had to continue teaching the class how to make pumpkin bread for Christmas, as everyone knows it's the best thing to eat for a Christmas morning breakfast.

...from me lately, but this one is really important.

Anna raised her hand and asked how much milk to add to the bread. I told her that we were adding oil, not milk to the bread.

Eva agreed with Anna that we were measuring milk not oil, so I sent both girls to the corner as well. The corner was becoming rather crowded.

Father, I need her. Please don't take her from me...

I pulled a perfect roast out of the oven and set it on Mrs. Davis' table to eat. Mr. Wilson leered at the roast, and I informed him that only gentlemen got to eat roast, and if he was not going to be a gentleman, he could eat gruel in the barn with the rest of the geese.

He let out a honk, but did as he was told, and I couldn't help but smile. The feast was going quite well and I was so glad that Grandmother was here to help me make it.

...too. Help me to understand Thy will, but please, Father...

Grandmother made the best things for Christmas. Her stockings were beautifully knitted. I never could knit as well as Grandmother, but at least my gifts were wrapped and under the tree.

Mr. Shepherd handed me a gift from the sheriff. I opened it and uncovered a new roll of gauze, and I turned to show Andrew how perfect it would be for our hospital.

...as Thou knowest, I want her to be healed, to be healthy.

Andrew smiled and shared in my enthusiasm over the ... the gift of gauze. He took it from me and set it in his prized bag of medical supplies and told me we were all ready to go.

Go? Go where? Where were we...

"Because, Father, I've come to rely on her. I -I need her...

...going? I wanted to keep opening my... what were we opening again?

"And Father, I love her." Andrew finished. "Please. Please, Father. In the name of Thy Son, Amen."

Twenty-four

t took more effort than I would have ever thought necessary, but I pried open my dry eyes. Andrew knelt next to my bed, his head still bowed in prayer. His hair was so dishevelled. I'd never seen it so unkempt.

With a great effort, I lifted my hand and felt his soft hair.

Something told me what I was doing would not be considered proper, but I couldn't figure out why.

He lifted his head. His blue eyes met my brown ones. "Lydia?" he asked.

"Andrew," I started. "Did you mean it?"

He looked confused. "Did I mean what?"

"You said you loved me," I answered, my voice sounding a little groggy to my own ears.

"Yes, Lydia. I love you," he said with the biggest grin I'd ever seen from him. "I'll always love you."

"Good," I replied. "'Cause I love you too."

He smiled at my sleepy tone. "I'll let you rest."

"Stay until I fall asleep?" I asked.

"Of course," he replied.

I drifted off. The last thing I sensed was the brush of his lips against my forehead as I fell back to sleep.

When I awoke next, Eva was sitting at my bedside.

"Can I have some water?" I asked.

"Sure!" she said and handed me a fresh cup.

I sipped it, letting it soothe my dry throat.

"Why am I not in the school?" I asked. If I wasn't mistaken, I was back in my room at Mrs. Davis' old house.

"That would be your doctor's fault," she said with a smile. "He insisted that you needed to be somewhere you'd be more comfortable."

I smiled, grateful for my sweet doctor.

"Where is he?" I asked.

"Your sister wanted news as soon as you started to improve, so he went to tell her. He should be back any minute."

I nodded, grateful for the information and drifted back off to sleep.

I woke to Andrew holding my hand. "You're back."

He nodded.

"Shouldn't you be with your patients?" I asked.

He shook his head, "You have a bit to catch up on, but we can talk about that later."

"Is it all over?" *Could that possibly be what he'd meant?* I hoped so, but I didn't see how it could be possible.

He nodded, "Yup, just in time for Christmas."

I looked at him, confused. Last I knew, Christmas was still a week away.

"Tomorrow is Christmas Eve," he informed me.

I felt a little like Scrooge on Christmas morning, finding out I hadn't missed the festivities. Although, I still had missed more time than I expected.

"Lydia," he started. "You knew you were sick. Why didn't you tell me?"

Didn't he realize? "You needed my help; I didn't want to let you down."

"I didn't need your help, Lydia. I just needed you," he said. The words came out as sweet as Christmas cookies.

Twenty-five

Christmas morning dawned bright and clear. I was still a little weak from my bout of influenza, but I was grateful to be able to celebrate with my family.

Glorious smells emanated from the kitchen. Anna had made another Christmas feast that I couldn't wait to taste. I had been trying to suppress giggles all afternoon as I heard her and Mr. Shepherd working together in the kitchen.

Josiah played on the floor, having captured a stray piece of paper that had been used to wrap one of his gifts.

I wondered where Andrew was. I'd been expecting him to make an appearance all day, but thus far, I'd been disappointed. I'd resolved to hunt him down if I had to. I refused to spend all of Christmas without him.

"Five minutes until suppertime!" Anna called from the kitchen.

I moved to rise from my seat on the sofa when I heard a knock at the door. My heart leapt as I hoped it was him.

Mr. Shepherd went to the door and let inside the visitor.

The visitor had made no helpful noise to indicate whether it was Andrew or not.

Then, all of a sudden, he was there. In the doorway to the parlor. A smile erupted across my face at the sight of my handsome doctor.

"I missed you," he said quietly.

"Then where were you?" I asked, a little harsher than I intended, but he just smiled.

He knelt in front of where I reclined on the sofa and pulled a small box out of his pocket.

"It took me all day to find it," he said.

My hands flew to my face as I gasped. Was that what I thought it was?

"Lydia Annette Miller, I love you, and I don't want to spend another day without you. Will you marry me?" he asked as he opened the box.

I squealed and threw my arms around his neck.

He laughed. "Is that a yes?"

Too happy to speak, I just nodded.

He placed the ring on my finger, and then we were kissing. Sweet, tender, beautiful. More beautiful than I could have ever imagined.

I loved this man. So much.

In many ways, this Christmas had been the hardest I'd ever endured, but it also would be the one I'd cherish the most.

I kissed my doctor one last time before we went to enjoy the Christmas feast, content in the knowledge that I could rest easy in God's tender care.

D e a r   R e a d e r ,

Thank you so much for taking the time to read my book! Words cannot express how grateful I am that you took a chance on me and my book!!! I hope you enjoyed it, and it helped you feel a taste of Christmas spirit while reminding you of the goodness of God.

If you enjoyed this book, I would be so honored if you left a review on the site where you purchased the book, Goodreads, social media, or anywhere else you can think of. Reviews help authors tremendously, and this author will be eternally grateful.

Sending hugs and hot cocoa,
Courtney Ranger

Gingersnaps

¾ c. shortening

1 c. brown sugar

1 egg

¼ c. molasses

2 c. flour

1 tsp. cloves

1 tsp. cinnamon

2 tsp. baking soda

1. Beat shortening, brown sugar, and egg until light and fluffy. Add molasses.
2. In a separate bowl, stir together dry ingredients, then mix with wet ingredients.
3. Chill the dough.
4. Shape the dough into balls and roll in sugar.
5. Bake at 350 F for 7-8 minutes, just until cookies start to crack on top.

Acknowledgments

This book wouldn't have been possible without the efforts of so many extraordinary people to whom I will never be able to express enough gratitude.

First, thank you so much to my amazing family. Thank you for providing encouragement, letting me talk out my plot, providing me with late night goodies, and everything else I am forgetting to list.

I am especially grateful for my wonderful mother and sister who provided much needed editing help! Y'all are the best!!!

Madisyn, thank you for everything you did to encourage me and keep me going through this project. Also, the cover is gorgeous! I love it!!!!

Abigail, you have no idea how much this newbie author has valued your friendship and your help with navigating the strange world of formatting.

Leialoha Humpherys, thank you for all of your advice and helping to calm down an overwhelmed author more than you realized you'd signed up for.

To my incredible hype team members (Katherine, Takaya, Sydney, Kyrie, Meagan, Paty, and Saraina), y'all made this project exciting and kept me inspired to write. I wish I could give all of y'all hugs.

To the wonderful authors of the Carols series, thank you for believing in me and taking a chance on me. I've loved getting to know y'all and have treasured the time I've spent interacting with you.

Finally, words cannot express my gratitude to my Heavenly Father who sent these wonderful angels into my life and gave me the ability to write in the first place. I pray He will use what I've written for His glory.

About the Author

Courtney Ranger has loved reading for longer than she can remember. She won her first national writing competition as a first grader and has been writing ever since, although she much prefers writing historical fiction and fantasy to essays about career aspirations.

When she's not preoccupied with a book of some form or another, you can find her masquerading as her alter ego in the local medical community. Courtney has a weakness for dark chocolate and has declared liquid glue her arch-nemesis.

Website, Newsletter, Goodreads

www.ingramcontent.com/pod-product-compliance
Lightning Source LLC
Chambersburg PA
CBHW031536310726
48971CB00008B/2499